PRAISE FOR HAZEL HOLT'S
MRS. MALORY SERIES

"Delightful." —*The Cleveland Plain Dealer*

"Anglophiles will delight in the authentically British Mrs. Malory, and mystery fans will enjoy Holt's stylish writing, dry wit, and clever plot." —*Booklist*

"Interesting . . . enjoyable. . . . If you haven't discovered Mrs. Malory, I highly recommend reading the rest of the series." —*Mystery News*

"A delight . . . warm, vivid descriptions." —*Time Out* (London)

"Irresistible." —*Yakima Herald-Republic*

"A soothing, gentle treat. . . . The literate, enjoyable Mrs. Sheila Malory is back." —*The Atlanta Journal-Constitution*

"A charming slice of British village life." —*Chicago Sun-Times*

"A delectable treat for cozy lovers, British style." —*Kirkus Reviews*

Mrs. Malory and Death by Water

A Sheila Malory Mystery

Hazel Holt

A SIGNET BOOK

SIGNET
Published by New American Library, a division of
Penguin Putnam Inc., 375 Hudson Street,
New York, New York 10014, U.S.A.
Penguin Books Ltd, 80 Strand,
London WC2R 0RL, England
Penguin Books Australia Ltd, 250 Camberwell Road,
Camberwell, Victoria 3124, Australia
Penguin Books Canada Ltd., 10 Alcorn Avenue,
Toronto, Ontario, Canada M4V 3B2
Penguin Books (N.Z.) Ltd, 182–190 Wairau Road,
Auckland 10, New Zealand

Penguin Books Ltd, Registered Offices:
Harmondsworth, Middlesex, England

First published by Signet, an imprint of New American Library,
a division of Penguin Putnam Inc.

First Printing, January 2003
10 9 8 7 6 5 4 3 2 1

 REGISTERED TRADEMARK—MARCA REGISTRADA

Printed in the United States

PUBLISHER'S NOTE
This is a work of fiction. Names, characters, places, and incidents either are
the product of the author's imagination or are used fictitiously, and any
resemblance to actual person, living or dead, business establishments,
events, or locales is entirely coincidental.

For
Brenda and John
with my love

Chapter One

"She's more or less dotty now, of course."

This remark, dropped into a momentary silence in the drinks party chatter, made me look around to see who'd spoken. It was Vernon Staveley. Other people had turned to look too, and he seemed embarrassed at having what he'd meant to be a chance remark made important by accidental circumstance.

"Well, of course," Vernon went on defensively, "she's always been a bit eccentric, but now—well! The village children call her Batty Nora—something to do with a television program, I believe . . ." His voice died away.

"How *is* Leonora?" I asked coolly. "I've been meaning to call in on her for ages."

"Oh, she's quite fit, I think—that is, I haven't seen her myself for a while, but Trish says she saw her in Dulverton last week and she seemed all right then."

Trish is Vernon's wife and, seeing her husband in something of an awkward situation (as he often is), she came up and briskly took him away.

"Really!" Rosemary exclaimed as we drove home. "What a way to talk about your sister!"

"They've never got on," I said. "And when their father left her that cottage on the estate, it made things much worse."

"Vernon's right, of course, in one way," Rosemary said, expertly avoiding a sheep that launched itself across the narrow road almost in front of the car. "I mean, Leonora *is* eccentric."

"Yes, but very amusing and highly intelligent. I mean, it takes a lot to be the foremost foreign correspondent of your generation, especially if you're a woman."

"Oh, sure. But it was rather odd the way she just left it all behind and ended up in that rundown cottage in the middle of the moor with only assorted livestock for company!"

"She just said she'd had enough. I should think the peace and quiet of Exmoor—with only the animals for company—would be a refreshing change from the sort of exciting and dangerous life she'd been leading! Besides, she was getting on. What is she now? She must be around eighty—so she would have been in her late sixties when she packed it all in."

"I suppose so. But she has rather taken things to extremes—never goes anywhere or sees anyone—and Anthea said that when she called last, the kitchen was really squalid!"

"I expect Anthea says that about *my* kitchen," I said tartly. "But you know Leonora—she could never be bothered about things like housekeeping. Still, I think

I'll try and get over there next week if I can . . . just to see how she is."

I've known Leonora Staveley for years, ever since I was a child. With long gaps, of course, when she was living in London or abroad on various assignments. But she always came back to Exmoor. "It's where I come home to," she used to say. "My refuge, my escape from the world." So, really, I wasn't surprised that when she finally gave up her distinguished career, she came back to live in the small cottage on the edge of the moor that had been her bolt-hole for so long. What was surprising, perhaps, and the thing that really puzzled people, was the way she gradually withdrew from society. At first one would see her at horse shows or point-to-points, at Dunster Show or even at the occasional drinks party. But almost imperceptibly she stopped going out and about. Now she only drove her ancient Land Rover into Dulverton (the nearest village) once a month for groceries and other necessities, and saw no one except the postman and, occasionally, the vet.

Some old friends still dropped in to see her, but, although she was never impolite, most of them got the impression that she preferred to be alone, so, after a while, they too stopped calling. There remained one or two people she seemed genuinely glad to see, and I was flattered to think that I was one of them. So on the next fine day, I put up some sandwiches and a flask of coffee and decided to go for a drive across the moor and call in on Leonora on my way home. My little dog

Tris, with the sixth sense that all animals have for an outing, was already waiting beside the car, and as I opened the door, he scrambled in and climbed over into his customary place on the backseat.

"Oh, Tris!" I said, "I wasn't going to take you! You know how Leonora's animals hate strange dogs! Oh, well, you'll just have to stay in the car when I get there."

It was a beautiful spring day, bright and remarkably clear, so that from the top of Porlock Hill I could see quite a distance across the Channel into Wales. I drove slowly over Porlock Common, enjoying the sunshine and high moor, empty except for the occasional small group of ponies that ambled unconcernedly across the road, only the foals stopping to look curiously at the car. After a few miles I stopped the car, and Tris and I ate my sandwiches beside the little bridge over Chetsford Water, listening to the skylarks and watching them as they rose higher and higher into the brilliant blue sky. Even Tris seemed spellbound by the perfection of the day and mostly stayed quietly by my side, only making occasional brief snuffling sorties into the dead clumps of heather when something of extraordinary interest attracted his attention.

After a while we drove on, through Exford and up onto the moor beyond until we finally came to the lopsided five-barred gate tied up with binder twine that guarded the track leading to Leonora's cottage. With some difficulty I untied the string and drove the car bumpily along the winding track through rough pastureland for about half a mile until I came to the cottage. It was built of gray stone, sometime in the eighteenth century, I should imagine, and was probably what's known in this part of the world as a shepherd's cot, because there were still tumbledown stone pens where animals might have been gathered in at lambing time or in the worst of the moorland winter. There were several sheds and an old lean-to, all in a state of disrepair, which added to the general air of neglect. Leonora's old Land Rover stood to one side of the yard with a large Indian bedspread draped over the bonnet, possibly to dry in the sun—the general effect was decidedly bizarre.

As always my arrival aroused passionate interest (and in some cases resentment) among Leonora's motley collection of animals. Two crossbred collies rushed out of one of the pens barking loudly, scattering the hens who had been pecking desultorily in the dust of the yard, while two goats, tethered on the patch of grass to one side, made strangled bleating noises and pulled at their chains, which rattled as they shook their heads, their baleful yellow eyes daring me to move in their direction. The other side of a broken fence, beside the stream that flowed along one side of the cottage, several ducks added to the pandemonium by flapping their wings and quacking excitedly. Only a black cat, lying stretched out in the sun across the path leading up to the cottage, remained unmoved as I stepped over it to get to the front door. The door was open but I knocked anyway. There was no reply so I tried again. Still no answer.

"What are you doing? Go away!" a voice behind me shouted. I turned quickly, startled by the fierceness of the sound and saw Leonora with the two dogs leaping beside her coming up the path. As she got nearer she recognized me.

"Sheila! Sheila Malory! What a pleasant surprise. Come in."

She led the way into the cottage, pushing the dogs, who showed an inclination to join us, outside again but allowing the cat to slide neatly past and into the sitting room, where it immediately ensconced itself, as of right, in what was obviously the most comfortable chair. The room was dark, since the only window was not only small with leaded panes but had obviously not been cleaned for a very long time. There was a large round table covered with a dusty chenille table-cloth and four heavy wooden chairs. A massive open dresser, filled with a miscellaneous collection of china and other household utensils, occupied one wall while the other walls were taken up by shelving crammed with books, upright, in horizontal layers or just anyhow in untidy piles. Apart from the only decent armchair now occupied by the cat, the other seating consisted of an unreliable-looking wicker chair, that had seen better days, and a stiff, black, rubbed-leather sofa (stuffed with horsehair that prickled your legs as you sat on it) that I remembered of old and consequently avoided.

I pulled out one of the heavy dining chairs and sat down at the table. Leonora joined me.

"Sorry I didn't recognize you at first," she said, lighting a cigarette, "but my eyes are getting bad and I keep losing those stupid glasses. They're no use anyway—I suppose it's cataracts. It usually is at my age."

"Have you seen anyone about it?" I asked.

"Oh, I will sometime," she said impatiently. "I can't be doing with quacks, as you know."

"Yes, but, Leonora, your sight—it's not something you can ignore. Especially living out here, you really do need to see what you're doing!"

"Yes, well." She dismissed it, as she had always dismissed any subject she didn't want to discuss, and I knew better than to press the point.

"So," she said, flicking ash in the general direction of a battered brass dish of a vaguely Oriental design, "how are you? And how are Michael and Thea? Settled down to married life I suppose by now. Any children yet?"

"Not yet," I said, "though I do long to be a grandmother."

"Yes," she said, "it would be nice to have grandchildren. I never wanted children, but grandchildren, that would have been good."

Leonora had never married. I suppose the nomadic nature of her job would have made settling down difficult. But she had had several affairs with influential men—a famous American novelist, a French diplomat and (some said) a member of the reigning house of a certain Middle Eastern state. I always got the impression (though, of course, she never discussed such things) that it was Leonora who, in every case, ended the affair, moving into another relationship as abruptly and unconcernedly as she moved from one part of the world to another. Although everyone— well, everyone who mattered—knew about these affairs, there was never any scandal. Indeed they seemed to increase her prestige rather than otherwise. She was primarily a newspaper journalist, though towards the end of her career she occasionally appeared on television, usually reporting from dangerous and inaccessible trouble spots, so that her name and face were familiar even to the general, nonreading public. But that was some years ago, and locally she was known as the eccentric sister of that Mr. Staveley up at the Manor rather than as a celebrity in her own right.

Leonora stubbed out her cigarette. "Will you have a drink?" she asked.

"It's a bit early for me," I said. "But I'd love a glass of your delicious water."

Leonora's water came from the stream that ran down from a spring at the top of the hill past her cottage to join the waters of the Barle in the valley below. Leonora drank pints of it ("Flushes out the system"), and I always said that it was so good it should be bottled and sold as a commercial enterprise.

"Right."

She got to her feet, and I noticed with a pang that her movements now were stiff and awkward, as if they pained her. She went into the kitchen, and through the open door I saw the sink piled with unwashed saucepans, the crusted animal dishes on the floor, and a general muddle of food and utensils on the large wooden table that stood in the middle of the room. I could well imagine that my friend Anthea, whose own kitchen was a model of hygiene and organization, might have been horrified.

Leonora picked out a glass from the pile of dishes on the draining board, gave it a cursory rinse, and filled it with water from the tap.

"There you are," she said, handing it to me. While she was rootling in the cupboard for the whiskey bottle, I surreptitiously wiped the rim of the glass with my handkerchief and sipped the water cautiously.

"Sure you won't have anything stronger?" Leonora asked, tipping a generous slug of whisky into another glass.

"No, really, thanks. This will be lovely."

"I've got some biscuits somewhere," she said vaguely, "unless I gave them to the dogs."

"No, honestly, this is fine."

She came back into the sitting room and settled herself carefully at the table, stretching one leg straight out in front of her.

"Stupid knee," she said. "All to pieces, stiffens up if I sit with it bent. *Anno domini*, I suppose, but it's a damned nuisance. And no," she added with a quick smile, "I haven't seen anyone about it and I don't intend to."

"How are you managing?" I asked. "Do you have any help with the animals, or anything?"

"Ted Hood comes up from the village when I need him, but I can cope—and I shall go on coping, even if it's only to annoy Vernon."

I laughed. "It's certainly an incentive," I said. "I can see that."

Leonora dragged a crumpled packet of cigarettes awkwardly from the pocket of her cardigan. "Guess what he's up to now?" she demanded.

I shook my head.

"He's going to sell the Manor and all the land to some property developer who wants to turn it into a leisure center—whatever *that* may be."

"No! Really?"

"So he's mad keen to get me out of here."

"But why does he want you out?"

"My dear Sheila, this place can be seen from the terrace of the Manor, and I don't suppose it's quite the image a 'Leisure Center'"—she put the words venomously into inverted commas—"would want, now, is it?" She struck a match with some violence and lit her cigarette.

"True."

"Anyway, they apparently need the cottage for extra accommodation."

"So what does Vernon want you to do?" I asked.

"He's got some sort of ghastly house in Taviscombe—a semi on the Porlock road. He bought it on spec a couple of years ago for letting. You know Vernon, anything to make a few bob! He wants me to move in there."

"No!"

"Oh yes. And—wait for it—he very kindly said I could live there rent free. He was at pains to remind me that I don't own this cottage and that Father only left it to me in trust for my lifetime. When I'm dead it reverts to the estate."

"For heaven's sake! What did you say?"

"What do you think I said? I told him—in the choicest vocabulary I could find—that he could stick his 'offer.' "

"Good for you! So what will he do now?"

"Not much he can do, unless he tries to make life so uncomfortable for me that I have to move."

I laughed. "Some hopes!"

"No, I've lived in some pretty peculiar places in my time and among some pretty hostile people, so I don't think Vernon is going to come up with anything worse than I've already experienced."

"Still," I said, "it's very wrong of him to do this to you. What does Michael—speaking as your solicitor, that is—say? Have you told him?"

Leonora stubbed out her cigarette. "Yes. As a matter of fact I did. He simply told me to sit tight—the law is on my side and there's nothing Vernon can legally do to break the trust and get me out. He also said to tell him if there was any sort of harassment."

"Good."

"And he also told me that the property developers

won't go through with the deal if they can't have the whole property—that is, including my cottage—so I've got Vernon over a barrel."

"Still," I said, "it's a rotten situation. Vernon is behaving very badly."

Leonora gave a short laugh. "It's not so much Vernon as that wife of his, Trish. *Trish*," she repeated the name scornfully. "What sort of name is that! No, she's behind it all. Vernon's a miserable creature, always was, even as a child. He wouldn't have the guts to embark on an enterprise like this. She's pushing him and she's a much more determined character; she won't give up easily."

"Oh, dear," I said sadly. "It all sounds horrible. I'm so sorry. You really ought not to be having this sort of hassle . . ."

"At my age?" Leonora laughed. "Oh, I don't know. I've always liked a fight—it keeps me young."

"That's true, but still . . ."

"You know me. Never one for a quiet life."

I laughed. "Not even now?"

"Never!" she said emphatically.

When I said good-bye she gave me a quick hug—something unusual with her—and said, "Come and see me again soon."

As I drove along the rough track that led back to civilization, I felt sad. I know we all have to grow old and lose our strength, but somehow it had never really occurred to me that this could happen to Leonora. She had always seemed so stalwart, an unyielding force of nature, but I felt that now, for all her brave words, she was uneasy and unhappy. The very fact that she'd spoken to Michael showed that. As I stood, tying up the gate again, I looked back along the track. It all looked so peaceful, idyllic even, with no hint of the stresses and anxieties that lay just over the brow of the hill. I gave the binder twine a final tug and got back slowly into the car.

Chapter Two

"It's perfectly simple, Ma." The note of patient explanation in Michael's voice was getting a little strained. "After all, if you can do something difficult like setting the video recorder, this is a piece of cake!"

I looked at the complex arrangement of towers and boxes and the spaghetti of wires trailing from the back of my desk.

"It's a bit more complicated than that!" I said. "Couldn't we leave it for today? I'll read through that splendid manual you brought," I promised hopefully.

"No, Ma!" Michael said firmly. "You're nearly there. Just run through it one more time."

After a great struggle I had reluctantly allowed Michael to drag me (protesting bitterly every step of the way) into the twenty-first century.

"You *can't* go on using that old typewriter," he had protested. "I mean, it's not even electric!"

"But, darling," I pleaded, "it's what I'm used to. I'm *happy* with it."

But I knew it was a lost cause. Once Michael makes up his mind to do something, there's no stopping him.

His father was just the same. So here was my very first computer.

"Goodness!" I said when Michael unloaded all the boxes. "Isn't there a simpler one—a computer for beginners, as it were?"

Michael ignored my question. "It's secondhand, so it's only half the price of a new one. But that's the great thing about computers. They get out of date jolly quickly, so you can pick up quite recent models for a song! Steve's just got a new top of the range one, so this was really cheap."

"How nice," I said helplessly.

I am not very good with machinery. My success with the video recorder was the result of many unhappy hours of trial and error and several long-suffering demonstrations by our nice television repairman. Like wild animals, machines can smell fear and they behave accordingly. Only a deep and abiding affection for my only child had persuaded me to embark on this particular odyssey, and I was already ruefully aware that our relationship might well be strained as a result.

"No, Ma!" Michael's voice rose sharply as my hand hovered helplessly over what was apparently the wrong button. "*Don't* switch off like that, you'll ruin the hard drive! Wait until it tells you what to do. It's quite simple."

I looked at the computer and it stared sullenly back at me. The possibility of it ever telling me what to do in simple terms seemed impossibly remote.

Thea, who had been very kindly watering my hanging baskets, came back into the room and took in the situation at a glance. "Michael, dear, I don't want to rush you, but we really ought to be getting back. There's several things I really have to do before we go to Jonah and Charlotte's this evening."

I have always said that a really sympathetic daughter-in-law is a gift from the gods. "Yes, darling," I said eagerly. "I'm fine now. I'll read through the manual and all that stuff you wrote out for me and have a good practice before you come again at the weekend."

Michael reluctantly got up from the desk. "All right," he said. "Just shut it down, Ma, like I told you."

By some merciful dispensation of providence, I managed to get the wretched thing closed down and they went away leaving me more exhausted than if I'd done a whole week's ironing.

"Goodness, you *are* brave!" Rosemary said when I gave her a vivid, if somewhat exaggerated account of my struggles.

"That is not the word I would choose," I said. "Fool-hardy, perhaps, weak-minded . . ."

"Oh, you'll do it," Rosemary said, changing her tune. "After all, quite young children manage wonderfully well. Delia," she went on, her voice softening at the mention of her granddaughter, "is marvelous and she's only eight and a half. She uses the one Roger has at home all the time, even the Internet!"

"Oh, well, children are practically *born* knowing

how to do those things," I said. "I expect all their genes are quite different from ours."

"I don't think it quite works like that," Rosemary said doubtfully.

"Oh well, you know what I mean. But I do feel that life is galloping on too fast for me. I'm beginning to wonder if I can keep up. Perhaps I ought to make a stand for the old ways of doing things, back to the simple life!"

"Like Leonora, you mean?"

"Well, perhaps nothing quite as extreme as that!"

"How was she, by the way?"

"Not very good, I'm afraid. She's getting too frail to live that sort of life."

"Frail!" Rosemary exclaimed. "But surely she's tough as old boots!"

"I know. She used to be. But this time I saw her— well . . ."

"Oh, dear."

"But of course she's still so independent—won't ask for any sort of help, won't go and see a doctor. I'm really quite worried about her."

"Not an easy person to help, certainly."

"She's choked off a lot of well-meaning friends— Leonora has never minded being rude to people!—so now there aren't many of us left who she lets near her. And I'm afraid that if I push things too far, I'll be out too."

"Oh no." Rosemary shook her head. "Leonora's always been devoted to you, right from the time when you and Peter were first married."

"Yes, that's true. She always said that Peter was the only lawyer she'd ever trust, and then, when he died, she stayed with the firm and when Michael joined them she insisted that he should handle her affairs, although he was far too junior really."

"There you are, then."

"Yes," I said, "you're right. She does need me. I'll go and see her again next week, but I'll give her a ring first in case she really doesn't feel like company."

This time when I drove up to the cottage, there were no goats, ducks or hens, no dogs even. Puzzled, I knocked at the door and a faint voice called out to me to come in. It was a damp and gloomy day, and there was no light on in the sitting room so that I could barely make out the figure of Leonora sitting huddled in the large armchair. She had a blanket around her shoulders and another one over her lap, where the cat was curled up apparently asleep.

"Sheila?" Her voice was weak.

I went over quickly and took her hand. "Leonora! What's the matter? Are you ill?"

She gave me the ghost of her old smile.

"Not too good," she said.

"Have you seen a doctor?"

She shook her head.

"It's nothing, just some sort of stomach upset. I've had worse."

"Can I get you something? A cup of tea?"

"A whiskey would be nice."

"A cup of tea first," I said, "then we'll see about the whiskey."

The chaos in the kitchen was even worse than before, so, while the kettle was boiling, I washed up all the crockery piled up in the sink and tried to tidy up a little. I found a rubber hot water bottle on the dresser, so I filled that too and took it in with the tea.

"Here you are," I said. "Try and drink it while it's nice and hot. And have this hot water bottle—look, I'll move the cat over so you can put it on your tummy."

She drank some of the tea and seemed to brighten a little. "That's fine, Sheila. I'll be all right soon."

I sat down on the sofa. "Leonora," I asked, "where are all the animals?"

"I couldn't look after them properly while I'm like this. Pat Jennings has them."

"Pat . . . ? Oh, I know. She runs that animal center on the other side of Dulverton, doesn't she?"

"Yes. They'll be all right there until I get better. Old Charlie here," she fondled the cat's ears, "he's fine. No trouble."

"How long have you been ill?" I asked.

"Oh, I don't know," she said vaguely. "A couple of days, I think."

"Leonora! You can't go on like this. You really have to see a doctor!"

She ignored my exclamation and said, "Those

wretched Bamfilde brothers have been making trouble again."

"Oh no!"

Jim and Eric Bamfilde are Leonora's nearest neighbors. They are middle-aged bachelors who somehow manage to scratch a living from a small farm whose land adjoins hers. While their widowed mother was alive, things were more or less normal. But a few years after she died, Leonora managed to offend them— something to do with whether or not a boundary wall was moved a couple of feet when Leonora had it repaired after it fell down—and they have been trying to make life unpleasant for her ever since.

"Oh, really! What is it this time?"

"Oh, a lot of nonsense about the stream. They want to divert part of it, some sort of irrigation scheme. I said they couldn't and now they're threatening to go to law. I really don't understand the ins and outs of it. They're completely unreasonable. It was all right when Lily Bamfilde was alive. She was a formidable old thing, but she was perfectly sensible to deal with. And she kept them in some sort of order..." Her voice, which had been made stronger by anger, died away.

"Don't think about it," I said firmly. "It's not important. What *is* important is getting the doctor to have a look at you. It's David Williams, isn't it?"

To my surprise (and dismay) she didn't protest this time, but simply nodded.

I found a telephone directory and dialed the number.

While we were waiting for the doctor to come, I tried to persuade Leonora to go to bed, but she wouldn't. She simply pulled the blanket closer around herself and leaned back in her chair. After a little while she was asleep.

Fortunately I knew David Williams quite well. He used to be the junior partner in a practice in Taviscombe and belonged to the same cricket team as Michael, so we greeted each other as old friends. He is a large, kindly man, the sort of doctor you always feel better for just having seen. I hoped he could persuade Leonora to take her illness seriously.

"Well, now," he said briskly, "let's see what's going on here."

He picked up the cat gently and handed it to me, and we both went out into the kitchen while he examined Leonora. I rummaged through one of the cupboards until I found some tins of cat food—rather more of them than of human food, I noted sadly—and opened one. Charlie weaved around my ankles as I spooned some of the food onto a dish. I stood watching him eating, wondering all the time just how bad Leonora really was. She must have felt really ill to have sent the animals away, and the fact that she had allowed me to phone David Williams without even a token protest worried me considerably.

After a while the door opened and David Williams came into the kitchen. "She's pretty bad," he said gravely. "I think it's some sort of food poisoning, but I want her to go to the hospital for some tests. I've rung the ambulance."

"Oh no!" I cried. "How awful. She never will look after herself properly. I should have come sooner."

"No point in blaming yourself," he said. "She probably wouldn't have let you do anything about it anyway. I've known Leonora Staveley for many years now, and I know just how stubborn she can be."

"Still . . ."

"Can you go in and see her now, she wants to speak to you. She was getting pretty agitated about the cat."

I went through to where Leonora was still huddled in her chair. She stretched out a hand to me.

"Sheila." Her voice was even weaker now, so I grasped her hand and knelt down beside her. "Sheila, I've got to go to the hospital—lot of silly nonsense—but I can't leave Charlie on his own." She leaned forward urgently. "Can you *please* take him over to Pat Jennings today?"

"Yes, of course I can. Don't worry about that."

"He'll be all right with the others."

"He'll be fine."

She sank back into the chair but then roused herself again to say, "The cat basket, it's in the corn house. Can you find it?"

"Yes, I'll find it, don't you worry."

She still looked agitated, so I said, "I'll go and get it now," and went outside.

The air was fresh and there was a brisk breeze blowing, for which I was grateful after the stuffiness of the cottage. I unhooked the door of the shed, where Leonora kept the animal's feed, and finally ran the cat basket to earth under a pile of old potato sacks. I gave it a good shake to get the dust off it and went indoors again to show it to Leonora. This seemed to calm her a little, and she was quite peaceful as I sat holding her hand waiting for the ambulance to come.

As the ambulance men took her out, strapped into a carrying chair, I was saddened to see how old and frail she looked and how despairing. As I walked beside her I tried to make encouraging remarks about how she'd be back in no time, just needed a little rest and looking after properly. She smiled faintly, her old ironic smile, and as they put her into the ambulance, she roused herself and said in a quite clear voice, "Look after my things, Sheila—everything. I'm relying on you!"

"Of course I will. Don't worry about anything."

"You won't forget?"

"No, I won't forget. And don't fret about Charlie. I'll take him straight away."

She nodded as if satisfied and they closed the ambulance doors behind her.

David Williams and I watched the vehicle bumping along the track until it was out of sight, then he said gently, "She'll be better off at the hospital. She really does need those tests."

"I know," I said, my voice slightly unsteady, "it's

just that she looked so weak and ill, so unlike herself. She's always been so strong . . ."

"She's not young," he said. "It comes to all of us eventually."

"I suppose so." I looked at him. "Do you think it's the end for her?"

He shrugged. "I honestly don't know. But, in view of her age, I think you should prepare yourself."

"I see."

He went indoors and I followed him and stood waiting while he packed up his black bag.

"I suppose I ought to let her brother know what's happened?" he said questioningly.

"I suppose so. Though I don't imagine he will care. Or yes," I went on with some vehemence, "he'll be *glad* if she dies, because then he can get his hands on this cottage!"

He looked at me in surprise.

"Sorry," I said. "It's a long story."

After he had gone, I looked around to make sure no lights or heating had been left on, then, picking up Leonora's keys from a dish on the dresser, I put them in my pocket and went into the kitchen to fetch Charlie.

Chapter Three

"So she's at the hospital, then?" Rosemary asked.

"Yes, David Williams had her admitted straight away, so he must think it's serious." I had run into Rosemary in the pet shop, and she was anxious for news of Leonora.

"Look," she said, "come and have a coffee and tell me all about it."

"All right. I'll just take this enormous bag of cat litter out to the car—Foss gets through *tons* of the stuff every week—and then I'll be with you."

Since it was early we managed to find a relatively quiet corner of the Buttery, and Rosemary said, "I'm glad David Williams is her doctor—he's really good. And so nice too."

"He seems to understand her very well. Anyway, he said he thought it was acute food poisoning."

Rosemary sighed. "Not *entirely* surprising, considering the way she lives."

"No," I said doubtfully. "But there were all those years when she was living in the most ghastly conditions in India and the Middle East, and she never got ill then. She was always fine."

"But she's been back for ages, perhaps her immunity just ran out."

"I suppose so. It just seems such rotten luck. She really did look awful when they took her away."

"Poor Leonora."

"I phoned the hospital this morning, and they said she was comfortable."

"Oh, I hate it when they say that!"

"I know. I did ask if I could go and see her today, but they said they'd be doing tests so she couldn't have visitors."

"I wonder if Vernon knows that she's at the hospital?"

"David Williams said he'd ring and let him know. But I don't suppose *he'll* go and see her."

"No, I don't suppose he will. When you go, give her my love."

The next day when I phoned they said at the hospital that she was "rather poorly," which I took to mean that she'd had a turn for the worse. This was very worrying. To take my mind off things, I gingerly opened the computer manual that Michael had left me, but I could make nothing of it. I found its casual assumption that everyone in the world (except me) was conversant with its own arcane language very disconcerting. Obviously my brain cells had been dying at an even more rapid rate than I had realized. I had, apparently, been left behind in the technical revolution. I looked at the computer with its gray-slab-sided tower and blank unhelpful screen, sighed, and put the manual to one side. I picked up Michael's notes and read,

Switch on the computer using the BUTTON on the front of the BIG BOX next to the TELLY screen.
WAIT for a VERY LONG TIME until the screen displays the ANNOYING PICTURE OF CLOUDS.
In order to write DEATHLESS PROSE double click the MY FILES icon . . .

Thus encouraged, I tentatively switched on and tried to concentrate. I had just managed to call up the file I was trying to work on when the telephone rang. It was David Williams.

"I'm so sorry, Sheila," he said, "but I've just heard from the hospital that Leonora died an hour ago."

"I was afraid she'd got worse."

"She just slipped away."

"Did they discover what it was?" I asked.

"They haven't had the test results yet. I'll let you know when I get them."

I went back to the computer and tried to work, but I must have hit a wrong key, or something, because suddenly everything went sideways on the screen and everything I tried to get it back only made it worse.

"It's no good!" I exclaimed to Foss, who was sleeping on a chair beside me. "I'll never get the hang of it!"

I closed the computer down and went into the

kitchen, made myself a cup of tea, and sat in front of the television watching the racing from Ascot until I felt more composed.

I phoned Michael that evening.

"I do feel badly about it," I said. "I keep thinking there must have been more I could have done—if I'd gone to see her earlier . . ."

"You mustn't blame yourself. You *know* how difficult Leonora was about people helping her. At least you were there to phone the doctor and get her to the hospital. If you hadn't, she might have died all alone and not been found for weeks, like some ghastly television program."

I shuddered. "Don't!"

"And all the animals are safely provided for; you were able to help her with that."

"Oh, goodness, I must phone Pat Jennings and let her know what's happened."

"I don't suppose she'll mind keeping them."

"No, she's very good." I suddenly thought of something. "Oh, dear, I've still got Leonora's keys—I put them in my pocket that day and just walked off with them. Perhaps you'd better have them. I imagine you're one of her executors."

"Yes. Edward's the other. So hang onto them until I see you. I don't suppose anyone will need to get in there for a while."

"I'm not so sure of that," I said. "I bet Vernon will want to be in there as soon as possible."

"Vernon?"

"Yes, he's planning out sell out to this firm who're going to turn the place into a leisure center—whatever that may mean—and he'll want to get on with things now that poor Leonora's gone."

"Oh yes, I heard about that."

"The cottage was only Leonora's for her lifetime."

"I did know that. But it's full of her things—he won't be able to do anything until probate's been granted."

"Good! I can't bear to think of him profiting from her death! Well, I know he will in the end, but not now, not before she's been buried even."

The funeral was very well attended. All her old friends—even those she had pushed away—rallied around to remember her. There were people from London too, and even a few from abroad. The old church was practically full. I sat with Michael, Thea, and Rosemary near the back, so I was able to have a good look at the congregation. Vernon and Trish sat alone at the front in the family pew; just behind them was a group of the local great and good old hunting friends; Harry Walters, a retired business magnate Leonora had known years ago in her journalist days, Edward Reynolds, her old Fleet Street Editor, and a distinguished-looking man whose face was familiar but whose name I couldn't recall, from BBC television. Rosemary nudged me.

"Just look over there!" she said in a low indignant voice. "Can you believe they had the nerve to come!"

I looked in the direction she had indicated and to my surprise saw the Bamfilde brothers, unfamiliar figures in their dark "funeral" suits. They were sitting bolt upright in their pew, looking strangely old fashioned, like something out of a Hardy novel.

"What a cheek!" I said. "After all the trouble they caused her!"

The organ that had been tentatively edging around something by Bach swung confidently into "Praise my soul the King of Heaven" and the service began. After it was over and we were all gathered in the churchyard by the graveside, I saw the Bamfildes had gone.

Vernon, who had been hovering around the grander members of the congregation, came over to us.

"Do come back to the Manor," he said. "We've invited just a few of her close friends."

I looked at Rosemary and raised my eyebrows and, almost imperceptibly, she shook her head.

"No, thank you, Vernon," I said. "We just wanted to come to the church to say good-bye."

He looked a little disconcerted by this but gave me a tight little smile and went back to the others.

"I hope you don't mind," Rosemary said, "but I didn't feel I could bear to hear him buttering up those people he considers important and being all hypocritical about Leonora."

"Quite right," Michael said.

"It would have been sickening," I agreed.

"What we should do," Michael went on, "is to go to The Royal Oak and have a drink. I'm sure *that's* what Leonora would have wanted us to do."

"A few of her close friends!" Rosemary said scornfully. "A few of the people he thinks might be useful to *him*. Networking at your own sister's funeral—how low can you get!"

"I think Leonora would have laughed," I said, "so perhaps we should too."

In the pub I said to Rosemary, "I thought your mother might have been here."

Rosemary's mother, Mrs. Dudley, the fount of all gossip in Taviscombe, is usually at the forefront of any event she considers to be of importance.

"Oh, Mother's decided she isn't going to funerals anymore. I think she feels that if she ignores Death in all its aspects, it may ignore her. Mind you, she'll expect a detailed account when I get back—who was there, what they were wearing, the lot!"

I smiled. "Oh, that's all right, then. She isn't loosening her grip on things."

Rosemary laughed. "No way. Actually, she'll be interested to know that Harry Walters was there. She's always said there was something going on—her words—between him and Leonora, though I never believed it myself."

"Your mother is usually right," I said. "And they do go way back."

"His wife wasn't there today," Michael said.

"Is that Daphne Walters?" Thea asked. "The barrister?"

"Yes," I said. "Very distinguished, his second wife, much younger than him. I expect she was in London."

"If you think of it," Michael said, "Leonora had a very full life and knew a lot of very distinguished people."

"Especially Morgan Jackson," Rosemary agreed.

"Certainly he was the most notorious," I said. "That particular affair lasted for quite a while—right up to his death, in fact."

"I never cared for his novels," Rosemary said. "Too macho for me. And he can't have been a very comfortable person to know—all that trekking about in Africa and the big game hunting!"

"Leonora was never one for comfort"—I smiled—"either in people or situations."

"Goodness, yes. Do you remember when she was kidnapped by those Nepalese tribesmen? I do believe they gave her up without a ransom because in the end, they were more scared of her than she was of them!"

"And when she left, they gave her that amazing kukri," Michael said, "a fearsome-looking object with a terrifying blade, but beautifully worked and decorated."

"She still has it," I said. "I mean, she still had it. Oh, dear, it's so hard to think that she's gone. But, as Michael says, she had a fantastic life—she traveled the world, she was one of the great foreign correspondents, at a time when women didn't *do* things like that,

and she wrote some amazing articles. I'm sure she will
be remembered."

"It's a pity," Thea said, "that she never wrote her
memoirs."

"Lots of publishers asked her," I replied, "but she
always said that that part of her life was over and done
with. Except . . ."

"Yes?"

"Except a little while ago, she did say that she was
thinking of it. She said she'd been making notes and
going through old papers."

"Really?"

"She used to laugh and say that if she ever did get
anything down on paper, several people would have a
very nasty shock."

"She must have uncovered quite a few secrets in her
time," Michael said thoughtfully. "After all, she was
one of the first of what you might call the investigative
journalists—as far as foreign affairs were concerned, at
any rate."

"I'd have thought most of the people she'd have
written about would be dead by now," Rosemary said.

"Yes," Michael said, "but their heirs and assigns
mightn't have liked the skeletons in their closets to be
revealed."

"Well, it's quite academic," I said. "Leonora's dead
and the memoirs will never be written now."

We were all silent for a while, then Rosemary said,
"It's best, really, that she died when she did. How she
was living—it would all have got too much. This way

she went quickly and she'd arranged for the animals and everything. Yes, it's just as well."

"I suppose it's what we'd all like really," I said thoughtfully. "Not to linger on in pain and misery, not being a bother to anyone. Yes, I'm sure that's what I want."

"Oh, really, Ma, don't be so morbid!" Michael said abruptly. "Come on, drink up. Let's have another round and then I'll order some food."

"It's funny, really," I said to Rosemary when we were driving home together (Michael and Thea had gone on to Dulverton to look at the secondhand bookshop there) back across the moor. "Our children won't admit that we're getting old. Every time I say I can't do something, Michael gets quite cross."

"I know," Rosemary agreed, "Jilly's just the same. They seem to see us still about forty-five, at the height of our motherhood, if you see what I mean. I suppose they can't face the fact that one day we won't be here for them."

"I think you start to see your parents at their proper age when you're in your fifties," I said.

"And then," Rosemary said, "you can't remember what they were like when they were young. I sometimes look at pictures of my mother taken when I was a small child, and I can't remember her like that at all."

I thought of the formidable Mrs. Dudley, who I had known nearly all my life. "You're right," I said, "it's impossible to think of her as a young woman now."

"It's funny," Rosemary went on, "I can remember

some of the dresses she had perfectly well—there was a striped Macclesfield silk one (whatever became of Macclesfield silk?) with short sleeves and a tie neck. But I can't remember her inside it!"

The afternoon was bright and sunny, and we stopped for a while just to enjoy the peace and beauty of the moorland all around us.

"Some of the ling is out already," I said, "and soon the whortleberries will be ripe."

"That's another thing," Rosemary said sadly. "Whortleberries. I adored them as a child, especially Elsie's whortleberry pie with cream, but now they don't seem to have much taste and simply leave purple stains all around your mouth."

We sat for a while in an elegiac mood, then I laughed. "Listen to us—change and decay in all around I see! Proper old women!"

"But it's true, though," Rosemary protested. "Things don't improve. What was it that Shakespeare said? 'We've seen the best of our time.' It's true, really."

"Henry IV, Justice Shallow," I agreed absently. "It just goes to show that everyone has always felt like that as they got older. I expect elderly Stone Age man complained bitterly about the wheel and said things would never be the same again."

"Well, they weren't, were they?"

"We only feel like this," I said, "because we've been to a funeral. Tomorrow we'll be back to normal, just getting on with things, not giving a thought to our own mortality. Thank goodness."

"Well," Rosemary said, "it does no harm to have a little brood about things. I wonder if Leonora did?"

"I think so. Just before the end. The last time I saw her—not the very last time, the time before—she seemed to be looking back over her life. I don't think she had any regrets."

"Well, that's the most any of us can ask, really."

The next day the melancholy mood had passed, and life went back to normal as I found myself busy with household tasks, washing the kitchen floor, taking Tris to have his coat groomed and his nails trimmed, and making a couple of Victoria sponges for the Red Cross coffee morning. I was just coaxing a reluctant sponge out of the baking tin with a palette knife when the phone rang. I put the phone down and went to answer it.

"Sheila." It was David Williams. "I thought you'd want to know. They've got the test results on Leonora. It seems she died of E. coli poisoning."

"What on earth is that?"

"A sort of bacterial infection. Young, healthy people can survive it, but, given her age and frailty, it was too much for her."

"But how did she get it?"

"We don't know yet. There'll have to be an inquiry. The Environmental Health people will be going to the cottage to do some tests there."

"How awful."

"She did live in unhealthy conditions, of course. All those animals—goats and poultry and so forth."

"Come to think of it, I seem to remember a thing in the local paper about children getting some sort of E. coli thing from a farm center they'd been visiting. Petting the animals and then not washing their hands before they ate their sandwiches. Would that be the same thing?"

"More or less, though this was a more extreme form. We'll just have to wait for the Environmental Health report."

"Oh, dear, nothing seems safe nowadays! How did our ancestors survive, I wonder, when you think of the lives they led!"

"There's a lot of common sense in the old saying about eating a peck of dirt before you die. Our immune systems are too refined nowadays."

"I'm sure Leonora ate more than a peck of all sorts of horrible things, especially when she was out in the East."

"But that was long ago. And she wasn't old then."

"Oh, *age*!" I said. "Everything seems to come down to that in the end!"

David laughed. "You could say that," he said.

I went sadly back to my sponge. It had stuck fast in the tin, and when I tried to prize it out, it broke into small pieces. Somehow that seemed a fitting end to a wretched afternoon. Then Foss jumped up onto the countertop and began to eat the fragments of sponge with apparent relish. It is a well-known fact that

Siamese cats, though rejecting with contempt and loathing any food offered to them in a normal way, will instantly eat anything they are supposed not to. "Oh, Foss," I protested weakly. But, thinking better of it, I abandoned the sponge and put the kettle on to make a comforting cup of tea.

Chapter Four

"E. coli poisoning!" Michael said the following evening. He'd rung during the day to say that he wanted to see me about something, but wouldn't tell me what it was.

"Not something I can talk about on the telephone," he said, which left me in a state of profound curiosity and frustration.

"That's what David Williams said it was."

"How extraordinary. Not something you expect in *England*," Michael said in what I felt was a rather insular way.

"There was that outbreak in an old people's home in Scotland," I said.

"But Leonora wasn't in an old people's home."

"Perhaps it would have been better if she had been. She might have been alive now if she'd been looked after properly."

"No, she wouldn't," Michael said firmly. "She'd have died of horror and boredom."

"You're probably right. Do you want a beer or a gin and tonic or anything?"

"Beer, please." He sat down at the table in the kitchen while I got out a bottle from the fridge and rummaged in a drawer for an opener.

"Right, then," I said, placing them with a glass before him. "What is it you couldn't tell me over the phone?"

"It's about Leonora's will. As you know, I'm one of the executors."

"And?"

"And she's left you all her books and papers."

For a moment I stared at him, and then I exclaimed, "Oh, no!"

Michael raised his eyebrows questioningly.

"It was very sweet of her," I said, "and I do appreciate it really, but, oh, dear, where on *earth* am I going to put them!"

Michael drank some of his beer and laughed. "I thought you wouldn't be too thrilled," he said.

"There simply isn't another inch for more bookcases," I said despairingly, "even here in the kitchen."

Every inch of wall space in living rooms and bedrooms that isn't hung with pictures is lined with bookshelves, all of them crammed full, many of them double-banked. We used to say, only half joking, that the house, being very old, was only held up by the bookshelves and if they were ever taken away the whole structure would collapse. When Peter and I were married we amalgamated all our books, except his law books, which were, mercifully, kept in his office. He too had studied English literature at Oxford before he turned to law, and so we each had volumes of the works of our greater English poets and novelists, not to mention all those books of literary criticism necessary for a proper appreciation of great literature, and neither of us felt inclined to dispose of our own copies, so we kept them all. Add to these the numerous modern novels we acquired ("Oh no! Not another book! You *know* what we agreed!"), my books on the theater and Peter's books on military history. Add too a great many of Michael's books ("I *will* take them away, Ma, honestly, but you know how little room there is in the flat"), which seemed fated to remain with me for all time, and it will be apparent that more books were the last thing I needed.

"You could put them in the garage," Michael suggested. "I don't think it's damp."

"I suppose so," I agreed. "But there's not much room in there either."

"I could put up some shelves," Michael said helpfully, "and there's an old filing cabinet in the office we were going to throw out. You could have that for the papers."

"That might do," I said reluctantly, "but, oh, dear, it's something I could have done without!"

"We really ought to wait for probate, but I don't imagine anyone will object if we go and collect them sometime next week."

"There's no rush," I said. "And anyway, we—*you* have got to get those shelves up."

"Actually, I'd like to get things sorted, well, the easy

things that is, as soon as possible because the rest of the will is—how shall I put it?—controversial."

"Really?"

"Mm." He nodded.

"That's why you couldn't tell me on the telephone?"

"Exactly."

"Well, come on!"

"You may not have known, but in spite of the way she lived, Leonora was really quite rich. She had quite a flair for finance, and given that she had access to a lot of useful information, she did very well in stocks and shares and so forth."

"She was a very clever woman," I said, "in many ways."

"Precisely. I suppose Vernon knew this, in part, at least. I mean, he knew there was money, and being her only relative, he assumed that she would leave it all to him."

"I can't think why he should think that!" I said indignantly. "After the shabby way he treated her. If I'd been Leonora, I'd have left the whole lot to a cats' home rather than let Vernon get his hands on a penny!" I looked at Michael sharply. "Is that what she's done?"

"Not a cats' home." He smiled. "Though, knowing Leonora and her love of animals, that wouldn't have been exactly surprising. No, she's left everything to Marcus Bourne."

"Marcus Bourne?"

"You know, the travel writer, the sort of person who does eccentric things in far-flung places—*Taking the Camels Through Uzbekistan*—that sort of thing."

"Oh yes. I remember, I saw a telly thing he did about trekking through the more arid bits of Spain with a mule. But why did Leonora leave him all her money? I didn't know she even knew him."

Michael laughed. "Nor did Vernon."

"Ah."

"He's talking about contesting the will. Which is ridiculous, of course, he doesn't stand a chance."

"So what does this Bourne man say about it all? I suppose you've been in touch with him."

"We tried. But he seems to be off somewhere. He wasn't at his address in London, and his publisher seemed to think he was somewhere in the Deep South of America."

"A bit pedestrian for him, surely."

"Oh, well, he may not be exploring, just doing a book signing in Montgomery."

"Well!" I said, tipping a little more tonic into my glass. "What an extraordinary thing!"

"She never spoke to you about him?"

I shook my head. "Never a word. And his name wasn't exactly liable to crop up in casual conversation. I wish I could have seen Vernon's face when he found out! And Trish's."

"*Not* pleased, as I said. Stunned, in fact. I think they'd been counting on that money so that they could go into partnership with this Leisure Center group—

more lovely money for them that way than if they just sold out."

"Of course, they'll get the cottage and the bit of land now," I said. "So they will be able to sell."

"True, but not as profitable as having an actual monetary stake in the thing."

"Well, good!" I said vindictively. "I hope their rotten deal falls through entirely!"

"Actually, it may, if there's any sort of health risk. E. coli has a nasty ring about it."

"You don't imagine Vernon will tell them about it?"

"I'm sure he won't, but there'll be plenty of people who will. Vernon's little scheme had some pretty stiff opposition from the locals, and there's bound to be a lot of fuss about planning permission."

"That's true. Oh, well, we live in hope."

Michael finished his beer and went over to put his glass in the sink. "So when do you feel like going over to the cottage to look at those books?" he asked. "Would Wednesday do?"

"Yes, that's fine. I'll start collecting cardboard boxes to bring them away in."

We bumped our way down the track, the empty cardboard boxes sliding about in the back of Michael's Land Rover. When we reached the cottage, it looked so desolate I could hardly bear it. Without the animals and, most of all, without Leonora's strong presence, the place was dead and dreary.

"God, doesn't it look miserable!" Michael said as we went up the path to the front door.

I noticed, for the first time, how shabby everything looked, the paint cracked and peeling. I gave him the keys and he opened the door. Inside it was dark and musty, as though it had been shut up for years rather than weeks.

"Just as well you *are* taking the books away," Michael said. "Everything will be growing mold in this damp."

The sitting room was just as I had left it, of course, on the day Leonora was taken to the hospital, and I saw with a pang that the ashtray with the stubbed-out cigarette ends was still on the table. Somehow this small thing brought home to me, as nothing else had, the fact that Leonora was dead and that I would never see her again.

"Some of the books are in here," Michael said. "Shall we start on these?"

Mechanically I began to take the books from the shelves and put them into the cardboard boxes. We packed all the books in the sitting room and in the kitchen.

"Do you think there are any upstairs?" Michael asked.

"I really don't know. I'd better go and see." I climbed the steep stairs and with some reluctance, feeling an intruder, I went into Leonora's bedroom. I don't believe I'd ever been in it before, and I was amazed to see how spartan it was. There was just a narrow bed and a table and one chair. No dressing table or wardrobe. On the table beside the bed was a clock and two books. I picked up one of them. It was Marcus Bourne's *History of the Silk Road*. I turned to the flyleaf and read: "For L. the onlie begetter . . . M."

The other book was one of Morgan Jackson's famous novels about life in Mississippi. The inscription in this was: "For Leonora—my last and best love—Morgan" and a date in the 1950s.

For a while I stood thinking about Leonora and all the years that had passed between the gifts of these two books. What an amazing life she had led, what extraordinary people she had known. In keeping these two particular books by her bedside had she too been looking back over her life? What had she been thinking in those last days? And what part, I wondered, had Marcus Bourne played—a part so important, apparently, that she had left him her not inconsiderable fortune.

I roused myself from these speculations and went over to the cupboard in the corner of the room. It was old and the latch was stiff, but when I finally got it open I found inside not the clothes I expected, but boxes of papers and photographs, piled high one on top of each other, filing the entire space.

While I was gazing in horror at the contents of the cupboard and wondering where on earth I was going to put it all, I heard Michael coming up the stairs.

"Just look at this lot!" I called. "There's tons of it—one filing cabinet's going to be no earthly . . ." I broke off when I saw his face. "What is it? What's happened?"

"Someone's been trying to break in."

"What!"

"I thought I'd better have a look around, so after I'd checked the downstairs rooms I went into the yard and found someone had tried to open the kitchen window. You can only see it from the outside because they didn't actually get it open. I suppose they must have been disturbed or something."

"Oh, dear. Village lads, do you think? Knowing the place was empty?"

"Possibly. Whoever it was, though, I'd better phone the police and then try and find some way of securing it. Goodness knows if Leonora had any sort of tools."

"Yes, she has. She rather prided herself on being able to do jobs about the house. I think I saw a box of tools in the corn shed the other day."

The local police weren't sure if they'd be able to come straightaway—shortage of manpower—but if we could secure it for the time being, then someone would come around and make a report and they'd try to keep an eye on things, though it *was* a difficult place to get at, especially when they had such a large area to cover, but, of course, they'd do their best. Was there, they asked as an afterthought, anything missing?

"*Is* there anything missing, Ma?" Michael asked.

"I haven't any idea," I said. "Everything looks much the same. But then, if whoever it was *didn't* get in, then I don't suppose anything will have gone.

Meanwhile, what on earth am I going to do with all this lot?"

Somehow or other Michael and I managed to carry down all the boxes from the cupboard and added them to the boxes of books.

"It's going to be a bit of a tight fit to get them in the Land Rover," Michael said, "even with the backseats folded down."

"We could leave the books for now and just take the other stuff," I suggested.

"What *is* it all?"

"Goodness alone knows. I haven't attempted to look at any of it yet."

"Well, you sort things out and see what you want us to take, and I'll go and have a stab at securing that window."

When we got home, we dumped the boxes of papers and so on in the garage and I firmly shut the door on them.

"Tomorrow," I said, "I'll worry about it tomorrow."

"I'll see what I can do about that filing cabinet," Michael promised, "and ask around about another. Though presumably you're not actually going to *keep* them."

"I really don't know," I said. "After all, Leonora was a brilliant journalist, and whatever she wrote would have some merit. I can't just dispose of everything. No, I suppose I'll have to go through them all and see what's what. There may be some library that would like to have them."

"Oh, well," Michael said carelessly, "you're an experienced literary executor—you must know the ropes by now."

When he had gone I fed the animals, who always expect something when I've been out—a sort of blackmail to punish me for leaving them—even if it isn't their official mealtime.

Then, deciding it was too late for tea, I made myself quite a strong gin and tonic and sat down in front of the television. By a strange coincidence they were showing a repeat of one of Marcus Bourne's travel programs on Channel 2. Unfortunately, I switched on almost at the end of the program and just found him trekking across a particularly depressing bit of desert with some unfriendly-looking camels. He seemed very young—he looked to be in his thirties—to have had any sort of relationship with Leonora, but there was the inscription and the fact that the book was by her bedside together with another book that obviously held great significance for her. I looked at the face on the screen, unshaven and grimed with sand and sweat, but a handsome face and somehow familiar, though perhaps that was simply the sense of familiarity one gets from seeing someone several times on the television. His voice was muffled by a sort of scarf he had wound around his face to keep the sand from blowing into it, but it was a pleasant voice and, in spite of my scornful words to Michael about his programs, I had to

admit that he was both knowledgeable and coura-
geous.

The music welled up and the image disappeared
from the screen, to be replaced by that of a young
woman with large dangling earrings chopping up im-
mense handfuls of coriander and holding forth about
the more esoteric aspects of Moroccan cooking. I
watched it mindlessly for a while, but thoughts of
Leonora kept drifting through my mind. Why had she
never mentioned Marcus Bourne to me? Certainly she
had always been a very private person, someone one
never questioned too closely about their life, but still, I
thought we were close friends, and if he was important enough for her to have left him all her money,
then why had she never spoken of him?

The woman on the screen was now stirring a large
pot of something or other from which the steam rose
enticingly. I was suddenly aware of the fact that it was
now quite late and I was decidedly hungry. I switched
off the television and went into the kitchen to make
my own less interesting supper.

Chapter Five

The next morning I cautiously entered the garage, leaving the door open in case Foss (who regards every closed door as a personal challenge) wished to follow me. I switched on the light and regarded the overflowing boxes with some distaste. Gingerly I removed a few sheets of paper from the nearest box and found they were letters from a highly distinguished politician. Others, plucked from the same source, were also correspondence, from well-known authors, newspaper editors, television producers, and so on. I almost groaned aloud. It was all highly important stuff that needed to be sorted, classified, edited, and finally published, and Leonora had left it for me to do. For a wild moment I considered jettisoning the whole lot and pretending I'd never looked at it, but some sort of innate scholarly conscience made me pull over an old stool and start to go through the papers more thoroughly.

As I did so, I realized that it was going to be a massive job. Leonora had obviously never thrown anything away—there was a letter from a well-known poet dating from the 1930s, side by side with a British

Airways label for a Concorde flight and a set of scribbled notes for an article on the Suez crisis and a menu from a Beirut restaurant with a smear that might have been blood or some delicious sauce. The more I sorted through the papers, the more I realized how priceless some of them were and how important it was that someone (please, not *me*) would have to do something quite serious about them.

I got up stiffly from the stool, switched off the light, and went back into the house. Then I phoned Rosemary. It's at moments like this, I always feel, that one needs the sympathy of one's best friend. Rosemary didn't disappoint me.

"Poor you!" she exclaimed when I told her about Leonora's literary legacy. "How ghastly! What a massive task! Do you *have* to do it?"

"I'm afraid so—well, I can't think of anyone else, and I felt that since Leonora left the wretched things to me . . ."

"Oh, dear, yes, I do see. So what are you going to do?"

"Well, I'll have to sort through them first, I suppose, and see exactly what's there. Everything's jumbled up together—I can't *tell* you! Anyway, when I've done that I'll see what sort of shape the book would have to be. Just a volume of letters, perhaps. Or maybe something more substantial, a sort of biography. I'll have to see. Then I've got to find somewhere that'll take the papers—some library. I don't know, perhaps her old college might like them."

"It sounds like an awful lot of work to me."

"I know, it's all a bit daunting. Anyway, I can't do anything about it for a while because I've got an article and a couple of reviews that simply have to be done first. So they'll jolly well have to stay in the garage for a bit. After all, Leonora's been sitting on them all these years, I suppose a couple more months won't make all that amount of difference."

"What you need," Rosemary said, "is something nice to take your mind off your troubles. I've got to go to Taunton tomorrow, something to do with some property of Mother's, so why don't we both go and have a lovely, frivolous shop and lunch at that new brasserie that's just opened. What do you say?"

"What a lovely idea. I've been longing to try that place. Mind you, it's very trendy. Do you think we'll be the only people over fifty in there?"

Rosemary laughed. "I think it'll be all right at lunchtime," she said. "I expect the beautiful people of Taunton only come out at night!"

We did the boring bit with Mrs. Dudley's solicitors first, and then settled down to enjoy ourselves. Rosemary and I have shopped together now for over forty years, and we have established a routine. If one of us wants to buy a special garment, both of us focus our entire attention on finding it—other, peripheral shopping comes later.

"What I've got to get," Rosemary said as we sat having a sustaining coffee before beginning our task, "is something to wear for this wretched Actuaries' Dinner with Jack next week. It's maddening that it's not long frock, because I could have worn Old Faithful for that. It's so unremarkable that I can wear it every year, and nobody recognizes it. I really can't *think* what I want!"

"Let's have a browse," I said, "and see what's on offer."

"I really don't think I can bear to try on another garment," Rosemary said, emerging wearily from the fitting room of one of Taunton's more expensive dress shops. "What do you think about this one?"

The saleswoman, who had been hovering in the vicinity, darted towards us.

"*Excellent*, madam," she said moving forward. "That shade of green looks marvelous on you!"

"Sheila?"

I shook my head. "Wrong sort of cut. It makes you look like a string bean!"

The saleswoman gave me a filthy look and moved over to a rack of dresses. "What about this?" she suggested.

Rosemary sighed. "No, I really don't want anything flowery. I did want something in gray, but there isn't *anything*!"

"No, dear," I said. "Gray was the new black the year before last, you're not allowed to have it now."

I prowled around the shop and found a silk shirtwaist in black with a pattern of tiny white squiggles.

"Here you are," I said. "The nearest thing to a Little

Black Dress. You can get away with wearing this one for *years!*"

"Oh, thank goodness," Rosemary said. "Just what I wanted."

She retired to try it on, and I must say it did look good on her. Rosemary is tall—I've always envied her height—and wears her clothes with an air, and the black and white looked really elegant.

"Oh yes," I said. "That's it!"

"An excellent choice!" the saleswoman joined in gushingly, happy to have made a sale.

"I shan't tell Jack how much it cost," Rosemary said when we were sitting in the brasserie. "Though, come to think of it, it's for *his* horrible dinner, so he could hardly object. Still, it's worth every penny if I won't have to look for something next year!"

"It's sad, really," I said, "what a chore shopping for clothes has become. We used to enjoy it so much!"

"Age, dear," Rosemary said. "More choice then. More things for *us.*"

"I suppose so," I agreed with a sigh. "Once you get past a certain age and, in my case, over size eighteen, then really we can't hope for much."

"Never mind, we can still come to trendy places like this without feeling *too* out of place."

The brasserie was certainly very smart, vaguely thirties in style, decorated in shades of peach and turquoise with lots of Art Deco mirrors reflecting complicated modern light fittings.

"It's very full," Rosemary said, "we were lucky to

get a table. Oh, look, we're *not* the oldest people here, there's a couple there—over by those weird-looking plants—who must be even older."

I turned to look in the direction she had indicated.

"Good heavens," I exclaimed. "It's the Staveleys— Vernon and Trish! And who's that with them? That youngish man."

"Just a sec while I put my glasses on." She fished in her handbag. "There, that's better. Good gracious! It's Matthew!"

"Matthew, their son? But I thought he lived in America."

"Well, he's over here now. Perhaps it's just a visit."

"Probably come to see what pickings there are to be had," I said vindictively. "Leonora couldn't stand him. 'Smarmy' was the word she used. Always trying to make up to her because he thought she might have power and influence in places that might be useful to him. She saw right through him and he knew it. So relations were never very smooth between them."

"Well, she won't have left *him* anything, then."

"No." I hesitated for a moment. "Look, promise you won't tell anyone, not even Jack, because Michael told me in confidence and I don't think it's public knowledge yet."

"Tell anyone what?"

"Leonora left all her money—and it was quite a bit—to Marcus Bourne."

"No!" Rosemary turned and looked at me in astonishment. "You mean *the* Marcus Bourne, the one on telly?"

"Yes."

"Well!"

At this moment the waitress, a tall blond Australian dressed in black trousers and a black and silver T-shirt bearing the logo of the brasserie, came up to take our order.

"Oh, goodness, I haven't decided yet," I said.

The girl gave me a scornful look and stood, pencil poised, waiting with a kind of condescending patience. "Oh," I said, flustered. "I'll have the Caesar salad."

"And I'll have the grilled goat's cheese thing." Rosemary turned to me. "What are you having to drink, Sheila? I'll just have mineral water because I'm driving, but do have some wine if you want to."

"No," I said, "mineral water's fine for me too."

The girl's scorn deepened several degrees. "Sparkling?" she demanded.

"Yes please," I said humbly and she went away.

"Oh, dear," I said. "I don't think I really wanted a Caesar salad." I considered the menu more carefully. "The monkfish sounds interesting. I might have had that. I hate cooking monkfish—all that horrible membrane—and it's no good all the cookery writers saying your fishmonger will prepare it for you, because he jolly well won't."

"I don't think you'd have liked it," Rosemary said.

"Look, it's down with eggplants and Pernod—sounds a ghastly mixture of flavors!"

"No, perhaps not," I agreed reluctantly.

"So. Tell me about Leonora and Marcus Bourne," Rosemary said. "What's the connection?"

"That's it," I replied. "I haven't the faintest idea. I didn't even know she knew him."

"How extraordinary."

"There is one thing, though." And I told Rosemary about the book and the inscription.

"They couldn't have been having an affair?"

"Good heavens, no," I exclaimed. "For one thing, she was nearly fifty years older than him."

"People do peculiar things," Rosemary said.

"Not Leonora," I said with conviction. "No, we'll just have to wait until he turns up to claim his inheritance. Perhaps we'll find out then."

"He travels about a lot—where is he?"

"America, so Michael said. I don't think they've tracked him down yet."

"Nice surprise for him when they do."

"Oh, look," I said, "the Staveleys are going now."

As I spoke they got up and were making their way towards the door. To get there they had to pass our table. As they drew level I said, "Vernon! Trish! Fancy seeing you here!"

They both looked rather startled to see us, almost as if they had hoped not to be recognized.

"Have you been sampling the trendiest thing that Taunton has to offer?" I asked.

Trish gave me a bright smile.

"We thought we'd give it a try, everyone's talking about it. The chef here is the one who has that television program. We thought Matthew might enjoy it; though, of course, *he's* used to New York restaurants!"

"Ah yes, Matthew," Rosemary said, giving him a good long stare, "are you over here for long?"

Matthew Staveley, dressed in what I took to be expensive Ralph Lauren casual wear, suitable for having lunch with one's parents in a small country town, gave her a version of his mother's bright smile.

"Not long," he said. "Just dropped over to see the folks." He had, I noticed, acquired, along with his New York wardrobe, a faint East Coast accent.

"How nice," I said. I turned to Vernon. "I gather Leonora died of E. coli poisoning. Have they found out yet where it came from?"

He looked annoyed at my remark. "I don't know about this E. coli business. Food poisoning, most likely. I can't say I'm really surprised. Leonora lived in really squalid conditions."

"Oh, I don't think it was straightforward food poisoning," I said.

"What do you mean?"

"Dr. Williams said there'd have to be an inquiry and the Environment Agency will be making a report."

"Such a lot of nonsense!" Trish said briskly. "It's perfectly obvious that Leonora was simply asking for all sorts of infections, the way she lived!"

"She lived like that for quite a number of years very

happily and healthily," I said. "It just seems odd that she should go so suddenly like that."

"I guess we all have to go some time," Matthew said, firmly closing the conversation. "We have to be on our way now. It's been great meeting you." He gave us the smile again and neatly removed his parents.

"What a repellent man!" I said.

"I know," Rosemary said. "Jack used to have to do business with him occasionally, before Matthew went off to be God's gift to Wall Street, and he took a very dim view of him; said he was into several shady deals."

"Like father, like son."

"Yes, except I think Matthew's much more clever than Vernon."

"That's probably why he's here now. Something to do with that deal with the Leisure Center that Vernon's trying to pull off."

"I expect you're right," Rosemary agreed. "Oh, good, here's our food at last."

"Vernon seemed very touchy about the E. coli," I said. "That's probably because it would put the Leisure Center people right off. But if there's going to be an official report, I don't see how he can get around that."

"Oh, he'll just say it's because of the animals or something. Or, most likely, Matthew will manage some sort of cover-up."

"You're probably right. Oh, dear, I do hate to think of that lot profiting from Leonora's death!"

"Still, they didn't get the money."

"No," I said, brightening up, "at least they didn't get that."

"How's your Caesar salad?"

"Wrong sort of lettuce and rather too many croutons, but at least they're fresh anchovies. How's the grilled goat's cheese?"

"That's fine, though I'm not mad about this red stuff, which I take to be the red pepper coulis, and it's all a bit meager."

I laughed. "Oh, dear, do you think we should have settled for an old-fashioned pub lunch?"

"No," Rosemary said firmly. "If Vernon and Trish can be fashionable, so can we. I think," she continued, "I'm going to have a pudding." She studied the menu. "Let's see what a really trendy bread-and-butter pudding is like!"

Chapter Six

In a sudden fit of late spring cleaning, I was turning out my saucepan cupboard. I'd just decided that there was no way I'd ever use a savarin mold again when the phone rang. It was David Williams.

"The Environment Agency has decided that the E. coli poisoning came from the water supply," he said.

"Surely not! The water there's always been absolutely marvelous. We always used to say Leonora could make a fortune by bottling it!"

"Well, that's what they say. They seem to have discovered a pretty formidable lot of coliforms and so forth."

"Well, it must be very recent. Whatever can have caused it? Was it chemicals, some sort of nitrate the farmers were using?"

"This sort of E. coli is usually caused by decaying matter—animal or vegetable—or animal droppings."

"What sort of decaying matter?"

"A dead sheep, perhaps."

I shuddered. "How horrible!"

"Country living, I'm afraid. These things happen."

"Yes, I suppose so. But," I protested, "people don't usually die from them."

"True, but, as I've said before, Leonora was an old woman . . ."

"Oh, dear, it does all sound so *wasteful*, such a stupid way to die. Especially for someone like Leonora, who's lived with real danger for so much of her life."

"It is ironic, I agree."

"So what's going to happen to the water supply now?"

"The owner of the land—that's Vernon Staveley, I suppose—will be required to provide a proper, approved water supply before anyone can live in the cottage again."

"Serve him right!" I said vehemently. "*And* he'll have to do it before this Leisure Complex company gets wind of what's happened. I hope it costs him the earth!"

David Williams laughed. "It certainly won't be cheap. And he may have to get planning permission if there's any new structure above a certain size."

"Better and better," I said. "That could go on for ages!"

"The longer the better. I expect you know, a lot of the locals around here are very opposed to that Leisure scheme. Leonora's death has been quite a blow to their campaign. After all, her occupation of that cottage is the main reason Vernon hadn't been able to go ahead."

"It was certainly very convenient for him. He really did treat her badly these last few years."

"Were they ever close? After all, they were brother and sister."

"No, not really. The age gap between them was so great. Leonora was much older than Vernon. She was off out into the world while he was still growing up. And then, with her career, she was abroad most of the time. She never got on with her parents—she said that when she was small they always made it clear that she was a disappointment and what they really wanted was a son to inherit the estate. Then, naturally, when Vernon was finally born, he was the blue-eyed boy and thoroughly spoiled, with the result you can see today!"

"Ah yes, I see. I never knew that."

"Of course, Leonora's—what shall we say?—*colorful* life didn't exactly endear her to her parents, who were very much of the old school. They hadn't approved of her having a career in the first place, and then, when she became successful and newsworthy, they were embarrassed, especially when the papers got wind of her affair with Morgan Jackson!"

"I can imagine."

"Actually, I don't think Vernon would have been so bad. It was Trish who really hated Leonora and did everything she could to make things difficult for her."

"Why did she hate her?"

"Well, Trish—stupid name for a woman her age, but I suppose Patricia wasn't trendy enough for her!—was jealous of Leonora's fame. She has these 'cultural' aspirations, as I'm sure you know, opera and avant-garde drama and trying to organize festivals of this and that. None of *that* went down well locally, though she's too self-satisfied to see it. And, of course, Leonora couldn't resist being satirical about it all— well, she couldn't bear any sort of pseudo art stuff. She was also pretty scornful about young Matthew. When he first went to New York—he'd only been there for about a month—and went on as if he was an expert on all things American, I seem to remember Leonora, who, after all, had spent her life traveling around the world professionally and really *was* an expert, giving him some fairly brisk set-downs. So, what with one thing and another, Trish never forgave her and was always egging Vernon to be beastly to her."

"Oh, dear."

"Oh, well, we must hope that the planning and environmental people make things really difficult, though I bet the egregious Matthew will find some way around things."

On Friday night, Thea rang and said that Michael thought we ought to go and collect the rest of Leonora's books, so wouldn't it be nice, if the weather was fine, if we took a picnic (she'd do that) and made an expedition of it.

"Oh, it *was* a good idea of yours, Thea!" I exclaimed as, with a chicken drumstick in one hand and a glass of white wine in the other, I looked out over the moor where the fresh shoots of the young bracken were just beginning to unfold. "It's a glorious day, and so clear! You can see for miles. I do believe that that smudge on the horizon is Dartmoor!"

"You can see why Leonora loved living right in the middle of the moor," Thea said. "After all the hot, uncomfortable places she'd been to, it must have seemed heavenly."

"Yes, she said that even in winter, when the mist came down or the snow blocked all the roads, and all the pipes froze, she still found it comforting and friendly."

"I don't think I could be as enthusiastic as that, though I do find it quite exciting with the mist swirling around, real Carver Doone weather! But on a day like this, I can't think of anywhere else in the world I'd rather be."

A seagull, who had been flying in circles overhead, landed on a large stone a short distance away and eyed us warily. Thea threw him a piece of chocolate cake, which he seized and flew off with.

"Oh, dear," Michael said, "now look what you've done. Chocolate cake! You've given him a taste of the high life, now he'll never be satisfied with a stale crust or a bit of decaying fish! He'll come back day after day, hoping against hope that the chocolate cake will magically materialize again!"

"Oh, don't," I protested. "I can't bear to think of a permanently disappointed seagull. Life is already too full of things to be upset about!"

When we opened the door of the cottage it all felt dreadfully depressing, so we loaded the books in the Land Rover as quickly as we could.

"I don't think anyone's tried to break in again," Michael said, shoving the last of the cardboard boxes into the back. "I've had a look around and everything seems okay." He slammed the rear door shut. "Is that it, then? Shall we be off?"

"There is one thing I'd like to do if both of you wouldn't mind," I said.

"Sure. Whatever."

"I'd like to trace the course of Leonora's stream, just to see—well, I don't know quite *what* I want to see. I know it sounds silly, but I feel I owe it to her, just to have a look."

"Oh yes, lets!" Thea said. "It's a lovely day and it'll be a pleasant walk even if there's nothing to see."

We set off across the field by the cottage and into a little wood. The stream seemed perfectly clear, the level was quite high and the water tumbled picturesquely downhill over pebbles and large stones. As we followed the stream along the bottom of the combe, the slopes on either side became steeper, leading up to the open moorland above.

"It all looks crystal clear," Thea said. "There's not even a lot of overhanging vegetation that might have fallen in and decayed."

"No dead sheep so far," Michael said. "In fact, no sheep at all. Shall we climb up out of the combe and see if there are any father up?"

But when we got out onto the moor, there were no sheep to be seen.

"I think," Michael said, "that if we follow this path,

we'll come out onto the road that leads back to the cottage."

As we walked back along the road, Michael suddenly said, "No cattle grids along this stretch, so of *course* there won't be any sheep."

"Why?" Thea asked.

"Without cattle grids there'd be nothing to stop the sheep from wandering goodness knows where, so farmers don't put them on bits of the hill where there aren't any."

"Of course!" I exclaimed. "That's why I can't remember there ever having been any around here. I *knew* there was something nagging away at me when David Williams went on about sheep and animal droppings."

"Could it have been a dead deer?" Thea asked.

"Not really. There aren't many deer this side of the moor."

We all walked on in silence for a while, then I said, "I can't help feeling that there's something odd about the way Leonora died. I mean, *why* was the water suddenly polluted like that? After all the years she's lived here—why now?"

"Oh, come on, Ma," Michael protested. "Not unlawful killing!"

"You must admit her death was pretty convenient for some people."

"You mean Vernon and the dreaded Trish?"

"Well, it was, wasn't it?"

"But, honestly, can you see either of them lugging a

dead sheep around and putting it into the stream! Come on!"

"It didn't have to be a whole dead sheep. It could have just been droppings—quite easy to collect up on the moor."

"Really, Sheila!" Thea protested. "What a ghastly thought!"

"Not impossible, though, you must admit."

"No," Michael said thoughtfully, "not impossible. But surely there must be other, simpler means of getting rid of someone. I mean, you couldn't be sure this would work."

"Maybe not the first time," I said eagerly, "but think of the cumulative effect. You keep on doing it, time after time, until it's successful. And the beauty of it is no one would ever suspect!"

"The perfect murder!" Thea exclaimed.

"Well, near enough."

"But who on earth would want Leonora dead?" Thea asked.

"Vernon and Trish and the horrible Matthew," I suggested.

"Surely not!"

"Well," Michael said, "I don't really believe that Leonora *was* murdered, but if she was, then I wouldn't put it past those two—three—to have done it. Vernon's a bit of a dimwit, a lot of talk and no real action, but she's something else!"

"A touch of the Lady Macbeths there?" I suggested.

"Absolutely. She was the driving force behind all

this Leisure Center business, with Matthew pushing hard as well. He's a nasty piece of work."

"Well, *he* couldn't have poisoned Leonora's stream," Thea said, "because he was in America."

"True," Michael agreed, "though there are such things as airplanes."

We were all silent for a moment, thinking about the implications of it all. Then I said, "Do you think I should have a word with Roger?"

Roger Eliot, as well as being married to Rosemary's daughter Jilly (my goddaughter), is a chief inspector of police and in charge of our area.

"We-ell," Michael said doubtfully, "you *could*. I mean, if you happened to run into him casually, you might just mention it in passing, as it were."

"In other words you think I should?"

"Yes, on balance I do. Leonora was a game old bird, and we were all very fond of her. If there's the slightest chance that her death wasn't just a horrible accident, then I do feel we ought to make some sort of noise about it."

It just so happened that I had two tickets for a piano recital, rather a fancy affair to be held in our local stately home, now occupied only by National Trust stewards, the family having moved thankfully to the Dower House. Cunningly I rang Jilly, knowing that it really wasn't her cup of tea.

"Oh, Sheila, how kind, but you know what I'm like at concerts—I fall asleep and shame everyone."

"You have every right to fall asleep," I said, "with two small children roaring around day and night."

"They do rather. Mother thinks I ought to make them go to bed at seven, but somehow it doesn't seem to work like that nowadays. No—but I know Roger would love to come with you. It would be a lovely break for him too; he's been a real misery lately. They've been changing over to a new sort of computer, and *everything* is absolute chaos. He's been so irritable about it all. A nice soothing concert would be just the thing."

"Oh, good," I said. "That would be nice. I haven't seen him for ages. He's so busy these days. Oh, tell him not to bother with food because there's going to be a buffet. With drink. Though, as everyone will be driving, I don't suppose there'll be much of *that*!"

I am always very pleased to see Roger, and he is kind enough to seem to enjoy my company.

"Lovely of you to invite me, Sheila," he said as we sat in a corner of the Great Hall with our plates of vol-au-vents, tiny sausages, and mini quiches that are such a feature of buffet refreshment. "I must say he played the Rachmaninoff and the Schumann really beautifully."

"It was good, wasn't it?" I agreed. "*And* the Chopin. I'm a sucker for Chopin, especially that particular prelude. It always reminds me of *Sylphides* and waiting for the curtain to go up when I was a child and we went to London for the ballet."

"Yes, music can evoke the past like nothing else."

"That's what Leonora used to say."

"Leonora? Oh yes—I was so very sorry to hear that she'd died. She was a great friend of yours, wasn't she?"

I nodded. "I've know her for years and I was so fond of her." I bit into a crumbly vol-au-vent and was silent for a minute. Then I said, "She died of E. coli poisoning."

"Good heavens! How did that happen?"

"The Environment Agency report said it was a polluted water supply."

"Oh yes, of course, she lived way up over on the moor, didn't she? What was the water supply? A well?"

"No, a stream. They seem to think that it was animal droppings or a dead sheep or something."

"How awful."

"But," I said, "Michael and Thea and I were up there the other day to collect some books that Leonora had left me, and, just for interest, we followed the course of the stream and there's no sign of any sort of livestock around there at all. In fact, there can't be because there aren't any fields up there—it's all open moor—and there aren't any cattle grids."

Roger regarded me cautiously. "So what are you saying?" he inquired.

"Well, it does seem a bit odd, don't you think? If it wasn't animals, then what polluted the water?"

Roger gave me a quizzical look. "Sheila, come on, now! Don't tell me you suspect foul play?"

"It's not impossible," I said. "Her death was very convenient for some people."

"A lot of people's deaths are convenient for some people," he said. "That doesn't necessarily mean that they've all been murdered."

"No, but . . . Oh, I don't know. It just seemed peculiar."

"It would be a very strange way of killing someone."

"But don't you see, that's why it would be so effective. No one would ever suspect!"

"Except you." He smiled.

"Yes, well," I said defensively, "I've visited Leonora in that cottage for years, and I've drunk the water there often—and very delicious it was too—and with no ill effects. But *now*, just when people wanted Leonora out of the way, her water supply is contaminated and she dies. You must admit there is just a tiny reason for me to be suspicious."

"Why do these people want her out of the way now?" Roger asked.

I explained about Vernon, Trish, and the whole Leisure Center business.

"So you see," I said, "how important it was for them to get their hands on Leonora's cottage as soon as possible."

"And she wasn't going to move?"

"No way!"

"Hmm." Roger bit into a rather dry-looking small triangular sandwich, examined it, and put it back on his plate. "I can see that her death may seem convenient for them. But," he continued firmly as I was about to speak, "that doesn't mean I believe that they somehow managed to poison her water supply."

I sighed. "Oh, well, I just thought I'd mention it."

Roger smiled. "And that's why you invited me to the concert? So you could mention it?"

"Of *course* not!" I said. "What an idea! You know I always love going to concerts with you. As for Leonora's death, I thought you might be interested."

Roger smiled again. "Yes, Sheila. Of course." He put his plate down on a chair beside him. "And if you do happen to follow up things other than the stream—just for interest—I'm sure you'll keep me informed." He got up. "Shall we be very adventurous and try that cheesecake? Or do you think the chocolate gâteau is a better bet?"

Chapter Seven

"Ma." Michael's voice on the telephone had that casual note that usually means he wants to ask a favor. "Do you think you could do something for me?"

"I expect so. What is it?"

"Could you come with me to that Actuaries' Dinner on Friday?"

"What! I thought Thea was going with you."

"She was, but she's feeling a bit off-color, so she can't make it."

"Oh, I'm so sorry. Is there anything I can do?"

"You could come to this wretched dinner. I really do have to take someone."

"It's very short notice," I said. "The day after tomorrow!"

"I know. I'm sorry. But you will come, won't you? Rosemary and Jack will be there."

"I know. I helped Rosemary buy a dress for it. And that's another thing—I haven't anything to wear."

"You've got masses of things. Wear that black one."

"That black one disintegrated several years ago."

"Well, I'm sure you'll find something. Thanks, Ma, that's really brilliant of you."

"So what's the matter with poor Thea?"

"Just feels a bit sick and grotty—nothing serious."

"Sick?" I said, "you don't mean . . . ?"

"Got to go now. Thanks again. I'll ring you about times and things. Bye."

I sat thinking for a while and then I rang Rosemary. "Michael's just asked me to go to the Actuaries' Dinner with him."

"Oh, good, it'll be nice to have a chum there. But I thought Thea was going with him."

"She was, but he says she's not very well. Feeling sick and off-color."

"Sick? Do you think . . . ?" she asked tentatively.

"Well, I did wonder. But I won't allow myself to hope."

"*Wouldn't* it be lovely! You must promise to let me know the minute Thea says something!"

"If she does."

"Anyway, it'll be lovely to see you both on Friday. What are you going to wear?"

"God knows. I'm just going to have a despairing look through my wardrobe. I really don't fancy buying anything new—there's no real time to go to Taunton, and Estelle is so daunting."

"Well, let me know if you need any help or moral support or anything."

"Bless you. I will."

I went upstairs and flipped through the dresses in

my wardrobe, hoping, in the silly way one does, that some wonderful garment that I had quite forgotten might be lurking in its depths. Nothing new manifested itself, and I was obliged to take out my one and only really formal frock. It was wine color (the fashionable color several seasons ago), crepe de chine with a figured velvet bodice and three-quarter-length sleeves. I put it on and was relieved to find that I could still get into it and do it up. "But only," I admonished myself, "if you don't eat much."

Foss, who had accompanied me upstairs, gave me a critical stare, commented scornfully in what I took to be Siamese, and disappeared into the depths of the wardrobe.

The dinner was being held in a large hotel, which had recently won several awards for its food.

"At least there'll be something decent to eat," Rosemary said to me as we all gathered before dinner. "Though I expect it'll all be small, designer portions."

"Just as well," I said. "I had a bit of a struggle doing up the zip of this dress, so I daren't eat more than a mouthful of anything."

Rosemary surveyed the crowd of people. "Not a lot of people I know and several I intend to avoid— Bernard Hopkins, for one."

"Goodness, yes," I agreed. "I once got stuck with him at dinner—he's the most terrible bore. I just hope I can avoid him this time."

Fortunately, when we went in to dinner, I found I was sitting by Harry Walters.

"Sheila!" he said. "What a pleasant surprise. Are you here with Michael?"

"Yes, his wife wasn't very well, so I'm a last-minute replacement."

"And very nice too." He smiled.

"Is Daphne here?"

"No, she has a case up in Durham and couldn't get away."

"What it is to be a successful barrister."

"Yes, she's done wonderfully well and I'm so pleased for her, even though it means we don't spend as much time together as we might. Actually," he lowered his voice, "it's almost certain that she'll be taking silk quite soon."

"A Q.C! Goodness, how splendid!"

We concentrated on our terrine of wild game (mostly pigeon) for a few minutes, then Harry said, "I was sorry not to have a word with you at Leonora's funeral."

"I did see you there. But we really didn't feel we could bear to go up to the Manor afterwards—not after the shabby way Vernon and Trish treated Leonora."

"Yes, I had heard. Rumor travels fast in the village. They say that she died of some sort of food poisoning."

"No, actually it was polluted water."

"Good heavens! I didn't know that. There wasn't an inquest, was there?"

"No. She'd been treated by her doctor for food poisoning—the symptoms are very similar—so no one suspected anything until the Environment Agency tested the water, simply as a matter of course."

"How dreadful. Poor Leonora. So ironic, really, after the adventurous life she's led."

"I shall miss her very much," I said, "she was such an old friend. Though, come to think of it, you probably knew her even longer than I did."

He nodded. "Oh yes, we go way back—early youth. Then we met again when she was foreign correspondent for *The Morning Post* and I was out in Iran—well, it was Persia then. That was just after the war. Then we met up again in Nigeria some years later, and we've been good friends ever since."

"Yes."

He regarded me quizzically. "You're thinking of the old gossip? Well, yes, at one time we were more than just friends, but that was many years ago and didn't last long. Actually," he said, "most of Leonora's little affairs didn't last long."

"I don't think she wanted to commit herself," I said.

"No, you're probably right. Except," he looked thoughtful, "except perhaps with Morgan Jackson. I got the impression that that was something special."

"She was very young when she met him," I said. "And very impressionable."

"Well, he was a remarkable man."

"Yes, so I gather, though Leonora never talked about him."

The waiter took away our plates and set before each of us a small piece of very pink lamb, decorated with ribbons of spring onion, balanced on a layer of rosti, which in its turn was balanced on a layer of spinach and something unidentifiable, the whole surrounded by dribbles of some sort of dark red sauce. Harry and I looked at each other.

"It looks very pretty," I said doubtfully.

"Perhaps," he suggested, "it's for looking at rather than eating."

"Well," I said, "I certainly won't attempt the lamb. I can't bear undercooked meat!"

"Oh, well, I suppose I've eaten more peculiar things in my time, so here goes." He took a cautious mouthful. "The potato's not bad, but can it be *beetroot* with the spinach?"

"Good heavens, I believe you're right. We might have expected it—I believe beetroot's the latest food fashion just now."

"Extraordinary! But to go back to Leonora and Morgan Jackson. I did hear that Leonora was thinking about writing her memoirs. Did she ever say anything to you about it?"

"No, well, not in so many words."

"What do you mean?"

"Well, she left me all her papers. There's a mass of stuff. I haven't had a chance to look through them yet."

"It sounds a formidable task."

"It is!" I said with feeling. "Everything's all jumbled up together. I'm very tempted to pass the whole lot on to her college library—she was at Somerville—and let them sort it out."

"No, you mustn't do that. If Leonora left them to you, then I'm sure she meant you to do something with them. I know she had very high regard for your work as a biographer."

"I must say I did feel a sort of responsibility, but quite frankly, I've got such a lot on at the moment, I won't be able to do anything about it for ages."

Harry was silent for a moment, then he said, "Look, if it would be any help, I could give you a hand—go through them and sort them into categories, letters, notes and so forth—so that at least you'd know what's there."

"Oh no," I protested. "That would be a dreadful imposition."

"No, really, I'd like to do it. Since I've retired I seem to have a lot of time on my hands. It would be interesting. I'd enjoy it, and," he smiled, "it would bring back memories of Leonora."

"If you're sure. It would be a great weight off my mind. Thank you."

"Where are the papers?"

"In my garage at the moment."

"Right then. I'll give you a ring soon and arrange to pick them up."

"I'm really immensely grateful."

"It's funny," he said, "how when you're working, you can't wait to retire and do your own thing, but when the moment actually comes, you can't think what that thing is. Unfortunately, I don't play golf or fish or play bridge. I still read all the scientific journals to give me the illusion of 'keeping up,' though I don't fool myself that I really know what's going on in that world anymore."

"So much more difficult for a man," I said. "Women never retire. Well, we may give up our paid employment, but we still have houses to run and meals to cook and families to fret about, even when they're no longer at home. Not to mention the ubiquitous jumble sales and coffee mornings!"

"Oh, I try to do my duty by the community, as they say, but sitting on the village fete committee and being treasurer of the PCC isn't exactly fulfilling."

"But surely you're up in London quite a bit, aren't you?"

"We do have a flat in Clements Inn—handy for Daphne's chambers—but it's a depressing place and I much prefer being down here. I just wish that Daphne could get down more often, but she's just at that stage of her career when it's important she takes all the briefs she can get, and she does need to be on the spot to see what's going."

"Goodness," I said, "it must be really hard work being a career woman. I don't think I could ever have done that."

"But you have had a career—all your literary work . . ."

"All amateur stuff, really. I've never been a proper academic—didn't want to, I suppose. To be honest,

I've always thought of myself as a housewife with a hobby. You could do that when I was young. Nowadays it would be considered a dreadful waste of a university education; we're supposed to want much more than that."

"Well, I think you've done very well. You did a splendid job bringing up Michael, especially with Peter dying so young. And your books are very highly regarded."

"It's sweet of you to say so, but, there again, I only write about people I *want* to write about, if you see what I mean. I don't think I could write to order—well, except for the odd review—not a real professional. Not like, well, like Leonora, for example. She was a professional to her fingertips."

"That's true."

"Do you remember that story she did about those mercenaries in Mozambique? And that one about the oil scandal in the Gulf? Or the one about petrochemicals in South America? Were you able to help her on that? It was your field, wasn't it?"

"Yes, it was, and I did put a bit of information her way when I could." He smiled. "Dear Leonora, she was unstoppable when she thought she'd got a story, like a terrier at a rabbit hole!"

"I can imagine. You are lucky to have known her on the job. I only really saw her when she was off duty, as it were. Anyway, your having known her for so long will be wonderfully useful for going through the papers. You'll know, far better than I would, who some of the people in her early life were."

"Her early life?"

"I've only had a very quick look through, but some of the letters seem to date from years and years ago. She obviously never threw anything away—though they're all mixed up with quite recent things."

"Good gracious."

"I hope you're not having second thoughts," I said anxiously. "It really is a formidable task."

"No, truly, I will enjoy it."

"I would like there to be some sort of book about her," I said. "She was such a remarkable figure, a brilliant newspaper journalist and then on television. I wish she'd carried on longer, but she said that television was the way in the future, and, although she did it so well, she never really enjoyed television reporting."

"No, she liked to do things entirely on her own. She said that even a small camera crew cramped her style. She liked to *infiltrate* a situation, take her time and get to know the subtle ins and outs so that she could wheedle information out of people. You can't get people to talk to you on those terms if you're pointing a camera at them!"

"I can imagine. She must have been immensely brave, when you come to think of it—a lone woman in that sort of world."

Harry gave a short laugh. "Oh yes, she was completely fearless. But that could get her into some difficult situations. In fact . . ." He hesitated, as if unsure whether to go on or not. "In fact, I more or less saved her life on one of those occasions."

"Really? What happened."

"It was a long time ago, when I happened to be out there myself before I moved on to South America. She was taken hostage by a group of rebels in one of the Gulf states."

"I never heard about that."

"No, the government kept it pretty quiet at the time because the political situation there was quite touchy in relation to Great Britain."

"So what happened?"

"I was out there trying to negotiate a contract, and it just so happened I'd had some contacts with one of the rebel leaders, so I was able to make a deal with him."

"And they let Leonora go, just like that?"

"Well, a certain amount of money changed hands— though, of course, the Foreign Office never admitted it—and, yes, they let her go unharmed."

"Good heavens! What an extraordinary thing. She never ever spoke about it."

"I fancy Leonora preferred to erase it from her memory as one of her less successful adventures. But she never forgot my small part in it, and it did bring us closer together."

"I should think it would! Well, that makes me even more grateful that you're going to go through those papers."

"I've got a couple of things on hand, but I'll be in touch with you about them very soon."

"Wasn't that a fortunate coincidence?" I said to Michael as we were driving home. "It'll take such a lot of the burden off my shoulders if he can just get them sorted."

"Yes, he's a nice chap. Mind you, I think he'll be glad of some sort of distraction with Daphne being away so much."

"I don't really know her, what's she like?"

"I've only met her a few times, but by reputation she's a bit of a smart lady barrister on the make. Fairly ruthless and determined to get on, one way or another. Lots of networking, which is why she spends so much time away. Poor old Harry is said to be quite besotted by her, but I think she only married him for his money and position. They say she was furious he didn't get a knighthood when he retired."

"She sounds a thoroughly nasty piece of work!"

"Let's put it this way, most people think he deserves better."

"Oh, well," I said, "if sorting Leonora's papers gives him some satisfaction, then we'll both be happy. I quite enjoyed this evening, though I'm sorry Thea had to miss it. Do give her my love and hope she'll feel better soon."

"Oh, she's just a bit off-color," Michael said casually, and I didn't pursue the subject any further.

Chapter Eight

"So what did you think of the food?" Rosemary telephoned me early the next morning.

"Very pretty and delicious in places, but I do wish they wouldn't make such an *effort* with everything. I'd really like to see things looking like themselves, not tizzed up in fancy combinations."

"Oh, I do agree. And that pudding with twirly raspberry sauce in fancy patterns, and the whole thing *smothered* in icing sugar! Still, it wasn't a bad do as such things go. I saw you were next to Harry Walters at dinner—that was a bit of luck, he's a sweetie. I was lumbered with Fred Bushell, not as bad as Bernard Hopkins, but pretty dire. Unfortunately, he's quite useful to Jack, so I had to listen to his golfing stories with *some* appearance of interest. But lovely to see Harry. Jack told me he'd been invited, but I didn't really expect him to be there. I thought he'd be a bit grand for something like that. After all, he was in charge of all the South American operations for one of the major petrochemical internationals."

"Harry's never really been grand, though, has he?

After all, he's a local boy made good returning to his roots. I'm sure he's a bit lonely rattling around in that great big house at Withypool while Daphne's in London. I think that's why he was there last night."

"Probably. It's such a shame, he really made a mistake when he married her. Paula was so much more suitable."

Paula was Harry's first wife, who died a few years ago.

"Sad, really," I said, "that they never had children. And now it's too late for him."

"Oh, I don't know," Rosemary said. "Men do have children in their seventies."

"From what I've heard about Daphne, it seems very unlikely that she'd be prepared to give up even a fraction of her career for motherhood."

"Poor Harry."

"Well, I've found something to cheer him up. He's going to go through all Leonora's papers for me and sort them out. And when he's done that, maybe I can get him to do a little more."

"What a good idea! How did you persuade him?"

"It was his idea, actually. I think he still has a sort of thing about her. Incidentally, you can tell your mother she was right, they did have an affair. He admitted it— well, he almost boasted about it."

"Really?"

"And he told me how he saved her from savage tribesmen." I told Rosemary about the hostage business. "But I don't think you'd better tell your mother that; I think he meant me to keep it a secret."

"Do you think that's when they had their affair? She must have been older than him."

"Fascinating older woman?"

"Probably. And one he'd just saved from a ghastly death. Irresistible."

I sighed. "What exciting lives people used to lead. How boring ours are."

Rosemary laughed. "Come on! You'd be appalled at the thought of trekking around the Middle East and Africa, let alone doing the sort of things that Leonora did."

"You're right, of course. It isn't that I don't want to see all these exotic places, it's just that, as Philip Larkin once said, I'd like to come home every evening."

Life went on as usual and, what with one thing and another, I was quite busy, but all the time doubts about Leonora's death were lurking at the back of my mind. So, when I had a free day, I set out for a trip over the moor. I took Tris with me, and my excuse to myself was that I was going to give him a nice run, but inevitably I found myself heading towards Leonora's cottage. The gate leading to the lane was now fastened with a padlock instead of being tied up with binder twine, but I parked a little way farther up the road and struck out across the open moor, Tris beside me, his nose to the ground following the delicious scents with which the open country abounded. I dropped down

into the combe and soon found myself walking beside
Leonora's stream. The path was overgrown, but as I
neared the land around the cottage, I saw that it had
been cleared; and farther on I came across evidence of
some activity.

Fortunately it was a Saturday, so there were no
workmen around and I was able to investigate undis-
turbed. It looked as if some sort of filter bed was being
made in the stream and a new collection tank built to
serve as a reservoir for the water supply to the cottage.
Obviously Vernon and Trish had lost no time in getting things moving so that the Leisure Center people
wouldn't know about the polluted water, or, if they
did, it would have been put right. I sighed. Whatever
the reason, the work that was being done had effec-
tively destroyed anything that might have been seen
as evidence in an investigation of Leonora's death.

I started back upstream again when a sudden
thought struck me. Leonora had said that the Bamfilde
brothers had been making themselves disagreeable because they wanted to divert the water for their own
purposes. As I walked along the path beside the
stream, I tried to decide which of the land on my right-
hand side belonged to them. I soon came to a field of
rough pasture with a five-barred gate giving onto the
path. This, I decided, must be Bamfilde land. The fas-
tening of the gate was heavy and stiff, and I couldn't
open it. So, very gingerly, I climbed over it, Tris
squeezing through the bars to join me. I stood for a
moment looking about me. There were no animals in

sight—in fact, I don't think the Bamfildes kept livestock anymore, relying on wheat and oats with some
of the ubiquitous maize and oil-seed rape to make
their meager living. I imagined this field, with its
docks and thistles, was subsidized set-aside and not
used for normal agricultural purposes. So why had
they wanted water from the stream for irrigation?

As I stood there, I became aware of a man coming
towards me waving a stick and shouting. When he
came close to me, he said angrily, "What you doing
here? Don't you know this is private property?" He
was wearing muddy overalls and had a sack tied
around his waist, and I recognized him as Jim Bamfilde, the older of the two brothers.

"Good morning, Mr. Bamfilde," I said brightly.
"Isn't it a beautiful day!"

Taken aback by this approach he didn't reply, but
stood clutching his stick more tightly and glaring at
me.

"Don't you remember me? My name is Sheila Malory and I used to know your mother." He looked un-
certain and I continued, "I believe I saw you at Miss
Staveley's funeral. That was a tragic affair, wasn't it?"

He muttered something about showing respect for
the dead, no matter what.

"I gather she died from polluted water," I went on.
"Do you share the same water supply? Have you and
your brother been affected?"

Apparently hypnotized by my manner and the tone
of my conversation, he replied in a reasonably civil

way. "No, tidn't the same place. We do get our water up stream from her. We didn' have no trouble like she did."

"I see."

"That fellow from the envirymental come over and says he's got to test our water. I says there's nothing wrong with our water; we've always drunk 'un. But nothing satisfies him but to take water from our tap and come up here in th' 'ood looking for God knows what."

"So what happened?"

"After nigh on a week he comes back and says our water's fit to drink. Well, I could 'a told him that, silly young fool. And we pays taxes for that!" he said contemptuously.

"I know," I said sympathetically. "It's a disgrace. I wonder," I added casually, "if you've come across anything strange in or around the stream—a dead sheep or anything?"

"Dead sheep? Was mean dead sheep? They're no sheep on our land, haven't been since before th'old man died. More trouble than they'm worth—and they'm not worth three farthin' these days. Who said there were dead sheep here, then?" He eyed me suspiciously.

"No, nobody said there were any *here* on your farm. It's just that the Environment Agency report said that the water might have been contaminated by a dead animal, and I thought a sheep or something might have strayed onto your land somehow and died in the stream."

He shook his head contemptuously. "Just shows what fools those envirymentals are. There wasn' no sheep hereabouts, and even if there was, what cause would it have to take and die in thic stream—no steep banks, nothing to get caught up on. Damn fools, don't know aught."

"I see. So you can't think how that part of the stream came to be contaminated, then?"

"No, I don't, and no one had better come saying we put nothing in the water, because we'll sue then for libel if they did."

"I don't think anyone is saying that," I said placatingly. "It's just a bit strange, the way Miss Staveley died."

A crafty look came over his face. "That's not to say that there wasn't folk who'd like her dead," he said. "That brother of hern and his la-di-da wife. They'd be glad she'm gone so's they can build their fancy *hotel*!" He invested the word with the most profound contempt. "But they'm going to have to wait and see— won't be easy, we'll see to that!"

"Good for you!"

He looked surprised at my response. "Aye, well, they better look out, that's what I say."

"I think local opinion is all on your side. Miss Staveley held out against it, you know, until she died. Well, thank you for your help."

I turned to go, and as if to make up for any show of

friendliness, he called after me, "Just you keep that dog of yourn under control!"

"I will." Although I had my back to him, I could feel that he was still watching as I walked back across the field and climbed awkwardly back over the gate.

I examined every yard of the stream as I walked back up through the woods towards the moor and the spot where I had left the car, but I could see nothing that might have been the cause of any pollution. As it had been when I walked this way with Michael and Thea, the water leapt and sparkled over the stones, looking the very picture of a pure moorland stream. Tris, finding a small pool that he could reach from the bank, began to drink. I almost leaned forward to stop him, but on an impulse, I scooped up a handful of the running water and drank it myself. It tasted cold and clear and refreshing—as Leonora's water had always tasted.

"It's no good, Tris," I said. "I really don't believe that pollution came from natural causes. Someone, somehow, must have *put* something in that part of the stream deliberately."

Tris raised his head from the stream and looked at me enquiringly, then shook his head, shaking droplets of water from his beard and whiskers, and scampered on down the path ahead of me.

As I walked slowly back across the moor towards the car, I thought about the Bamfilde brothers. From what I had seen of their land, there seemed no earthly reason why they should have wanted to take water from the stream for irrigation. I turned the problem over in my mind, without coming to any sensible conclusion. Probably the whole things was just part of the ongoing feud they seemed to have had with Leonora. I couldn't remember *how* it had started, though, given their touchiness and generally suspicious natures and Leonora's outspokenness, it wasn't hard to see how such a state of affairs might have come into being. Could they have had anything to do with Leonora's death? They certainly had the means and opportunity to put something in the water, but although in many ways they seemed to be living in the nineteenth century, I could hardly believe that they would go in for the kind of revenge that one would expect to find in the most melodramatic kind of novel about Victorian agricultural passions.

I tried to put the whole subject out of my mind and to concentrate on the beauties of the day and the glories of the landscape. The sky was brilliantly blue with just a few feathery clouds, and the sun was really warm on my face. The moor was looking at its best with the gorse and the early ling, brighter than the later heather, lighting up the landscape with patches of brilliant cerise and gold. A skylark started up from the ground near my feet and soared into the bright air, and I felt at one with all the nature poets I had ever read and wonderfully at peace.

Just ahead of me Tris was barking excitedly, and as I came up to him I saw to my horror that he had come upon a snake, its thick dark body curled around an old dead heather root. I saw the telltale zigzag markings of the adder, and in a panic I snatched Tris away and ran with him to the car, slamming the door and, idiotically, locking it as well. I was trembling, my heart was thumping, and I felt sick.

"Oh, Tris! Oh, Tris!" I kept repeating stupidly while he, although worried by my distress, had no idea how near to death he had been. Eventually I pulled myself together and drove very slowly home.

The phone was ringing as I opened the front door. It was Thea, and the news she had for me was enough to drive any thoughts of Leonora, the Bamfildes and even the adder out of my head. We had a long and very satisfactory conversation, at the end of which I asked, "Can I tell Rosemary?"

"Of course you can. We're so thrilled, we want everyone to know."

"Even Mrs. Dudley?"

Thea laughed. "I expect Mrs. Dudley knew before we did!"

Rosemary was almost as delighted as me.

"Welcome to the club," she said. "When's it due?"

"Mid February, so it'll be a winter baby. I'd better start knitting little woolly garments right away!"

"Don't go mad," Rosemary said. "I knitted masses of stuff for Delia before she was born, and she hardly wore any of them, she grew so quickly!"

"Oh, well," I said. "It will keep me occupied."

"What about all that stuff of Leonora's?"

"Oh, that. I'll leave most of that to Harry. This is far more important!"

"Spoken like a true grandmother."

"It's funny," I said, "but almost the last time I saw Leonora, she said she wished she could have been a grandmother."

"She'd have been a jolly interesting one!"

"Goodness, yes. And a subversive one, too, always egging the child on to do something dashing its parents wouldn't have approved of."

"So is Thea going to go on working?" Rosemary asked. "After, I mean."

"No, she said she wanted to stay at home and look after the baby. She's very good at her job, but I don't think she's really a career girl. And then, of course, they'll have to look for a house. That flat is very nice, and there is a spare room they can use as a nursery. Fortunately it's a ground-floor flat, so it'll be all right about the pram, but there's no proper garden . . ." I broke off and said, "Oh, dear, I have a terrible feeling I'm going to become a ghastly baby bore!"

Rosemary laughed. "It's all right, dear, we all go through that phase. It does wear off after a bit. Now, the important thing is, do I tell Mother?"

"Oh yes, Thea was simply bubbling over with excitement. I got the feeling that she was half inclined to put an announcement in the *Free Press*!"

When I had finished talking to Rosemary, I felt very tired. It had certainly been an eventful day, what with Jim Bamfilde and the adder and then Thea's wonder-

ful news. I didn't have the energy to make myself a
proper supper, so I simply had a boiled egg and some
bread and butter. When I had eaten that, I sat in front
of the television with the animals (Tris safely tucked
up beside me on the sofa and Foss on my lap) and
slept through the programs until the loud insistent
music of the late news woke me, and I dragged myself
reluctantly to my feet, switched the set off, sorted out
the animals, and went to bed.

Just before I fell asleep, the picture came into my
mind again of the snake curled round the heather root
in the middle of the moor, and I thought, in a muddled
sort of way, of how I had been reminded sharply that
even in the midst of peace and beauty danger lurked,
and that, although Leonora had come home to the
tranquil English countryside after all her adventures
in harsh and exotic places, it was that same peaceful
countryside that had killed her in the end.

Chapter Nine

Since there is no longer a wool shop in Taviscombe and I simply couldn't wait to start knitting small garments, the next day I went into Taunton. Loaded down with lemon, pale green, and white baby wool, knitting needles (why can one never find the right size needles among the scores of loose ones lying about in drawers?) and patterns, I decided I was badly in need of some refreshment. I went into one of the newly opened coffee places and, rejecting the incredible varieties of coffee on offer, settled for a hot chocolate, which I took to the only empty table in the far corner. I extracted one of the knitting patterns from the bag and was just examining it and wondering if I was really up to executing the complicated stitches it seemed to require, when a voice behind me said, "Hello, Sheila. Do you mind if I join you?" It was David Williams.

"Good gracious, fancy seeing you here!" I exclaimed.

"I've got a meeting in about an hour. There was an extraordinary lack of traffic and I'm frightfully early, so I thought I'd fill in time. Nice to have company. What brings you to Taunton—shopping?"

I explained my mission and the reason for it.

"How splendid! Give them both my congratulations. We could do with some good news—I'm still upset about poor Leonora and the way she died."

"It wasn't something anyone could have predicted. I mean, food poisoning was always a possibility, given the way Leonora lived, but no one had any suspicion about the water supply."

"No, that was odd."

"I was talking to Jim Bamfilde," I said, "and apparently their water was perfectly all right. They live higher up, of course, so whatever it was that polluted it must have been in that part of the stream between their farm and Leonora's. Do you know if the environmental people found anything?"

"No, they didn't—at least they haven't told me if they did, and I'm pretty sure they would have done."

"Ah."

He looked at me enquiringly. "Ah? Do you have thoughts on the matter?"

I took a sip of my chocolate and decided to confide in David Williams. "Well, yes," I said. "It seems to me that there was something very peculiar about the whole business."

"Really?"

"The environmental people said it was probably animal droppings or a dead animal that contaminated the water, but there aren't any sheep up there. Jim Bamfilde said as much, and I checked for myself."

"Deer, then?"

"Not in that part of the moor, nor ponies."

"I could have been decaying vegetable matter."

"Michael, Thea, and I followed the length of that stream between the Bamfilde's and Leonora's cottage and examined it pretty thoroughly, and there was no sign of anything there. Besides, I'm sure the environmental people had a jolly good look, and it doesn't sound as if they've come up with anything, either. Actually, it's just as well we looked when we did because I was up there yesterday and Vernon's had a new filter bed and tank made, which will have destroyed any evidence."

David Williams looked at me sharply. "Evidence? Do you think there's been some sort of foul play, then?"

"It's beginning to look like it," I said.

He was silent for a moment then, leaning forward slightly, he said earnestly, "Look, Sheila, I know it looks peculiar to you but, believe me, these things do happen. I know how fond you were of Leonora and how upset you must have been about her death, but you should really try to accept it and let it go."

"No, it isn't that, really. It's just that I can't get it out of my mind how very convenient it was for some people that Leonora died when she did."

"You mean Vernon, of course."

"Well, don't you agree?"

He shrugged. "That's as may be, but I really don't think you should go around accusing him of murder!"

"I'm not the only one," I said defensively. "Mind you, it might be difficult to prove. We don't have an actual *time* for which people might need alibis. I imagine the poisoning, if that's what it was, took place over a period."

He looked thoughtful. "Well, actually, that's not quite true," he said.

"Oh?"

"It seems that there must have been a massive build up of E. coli over a short period, perhaps just one day. Then the effect of the bacteria was diluted by the progress of the stream."

"But how do they know that, if they didn't test the water until after she died?"

"Remember the tests they did when Leonora first went into hospital? The E. coli bacteria stay in the body for up to three days, so they were able to work out the progress of the contamination by comparing those results with the water testing they did a few days later."

"I see. So when was the crucial day when all this might have happened?"

"It must have been the day before you found her, which was a Thursday—so that would be Wednesday the twenty-third. But I don't really think it will ever be possible to prove that anything other than natural causes was behind Leonora's death." He looked at his watch. "Well, I suppose I ought to be getting on. It was

good to see you. But, Sheila"—here he regarded me seriously—"do be careful what you say. I mean, Vernon
isn't going to be very pleased if he hears the sort of
things you've been accusing him of, and, while I don't
believe he'd actually sue you, he might take some sort
of action."

"It's all right, David, I'll only share my views with
like-minded people, like you!"

He laughed and, with a wave of his hand, he was
gone.

I sat for a while thinking about what he had said.
Now I had an actual date to work on, it seemed to me
that at least I could make a stab at checking the alibis
of the people who might have been involved, though
how I'd be able to go about it I couldn't for the moment imagine.

"So you see," I said to Thea, "it does give me *something* to go on."

Thea had come around one evening to see which of
the patterns she liked so that I could make a start.

"Mm, I suppose so. But how will you do it? I mean,
you can hardly ask people."

"Oh," I said vaguely, "I daresay the information
will come out naturally." I picked out one of the patterns and held it up.

"What about this one with the matching leggings?"

"Oh yes, I like that. Of course the flat will be perfectly warm, but if we have a cold winter, that pram set
will be perfect."

"Good, it's just stocking stitch and moss stitch. I can manage those quite easily. What do you think, lemon or pale green?"

"I think the pale green, don't you?"

"Talking of the flat," I said, putting the pattern to one side with some balls of the appropriate wool, "have you done anything about looking for a house yet?"

"Oh, lots of estate agents' brochures, but nothing we really liked. Except one just outside Porlock that looks quite nice. I've got an order to view tomorrow, actually. Do you feel like coming with me? Michael's working so he can't come, and I'd like another opinion."

"I'd love to," I said enthusiastically.

The house (solidly built, early 1930s) was set back far from the road in a big garden.

"It looks nice," Thea said. "And it's a very quiet road so I won't have to worry too much about Smoke and the traffic. She *will* go across the road from the flat—there's another cat in one of the houses opposite she likes to visit—and the cars do come down that bit of West Hill quite fast. This will be much safer."

The woman who opened the door looked familiar, but I couldn't place her until she said, "It's Mrs. Malory, isn't it? Mrs. Sheila Malory, that is." She smiled at Thea. "And this, Mrs. Malory, must be your daughter-in-law, Michael's wife. I saw the announcement of the wedding in the *Free Press*. I don't expect you remember me, but we—my late husband and I—used to have the newsagents next to your husband's office in the Parade."

"Of course I remember! It's Mrs. Freeman! I didn't know your husband had died. I'm so sorry."

"It was two years ago now. We'd been retired for some time, though. Won't you both come through— would you like a cup of tea? No, it's no trouble, I was just going to have one myself. It's really nice to have a bit of company. I do find it gets lonely. That's really why I'm selling up and going to live near my daughter at Dulverton. Well, there's nothing like your own family is there, when you're getting on . . ."

She led the way, still talking, into a pleasant sitting room with doors leading out to the garden. "Do sit down, I'll just go and put the kettle on."

Thea and I exchanged smiles, and I looked around me. The room was basically large and light but seemed smaller than it was because of the amazing amount of furniture that had been crammed in it. There were two sofas, two large armchairs, a folded-down gate-legged table, a nest of smaller tables, an enormous mahogany sideboard, and set around the edges of the room were at least ten upright chairs standing guard, as it were, over the rest. As far as one could tell, the walls were papered in a sort of lime green, but they were so covered in pictures that only glimpses of the color could be seen. The pictures were mostly watercolors of local scenes, with here and there a carefully composed still

life, all obviously amateur work but, nevertheless,
showing some talent.

"Goodness," Thea said, "what a lot of pictures! And
all, I think, by the same hand. Surely not Mrs. Freeman?"

At that moment Mrs. Freeman came bursting back
into the room, bearing a tray with tea things and an
enormous sponge cake. "Wasn't that fortunate," she
said, "I made one of my coffee sponges only this morning or there are some almond tarts if you'd rather."

"The sponge looks lovely," I said.

"We were just admiring your pictures," Thea said.

"Oh, that was Will's little hobby. Always out painting, in all winds and weathers."

I got up and went to look at one of the paintings. "I
believe I know where this was done," I said. "It's near
Dulverton, isn't it? My friend Leonora Staveley had a
cottage just beyond this little wood. I recognize the
gate leading down to the track where she lived."

"That's right!" Mrs. Freeman turned to regard me
with some surprise. "Fancy you knowing Miss Staveley!"

"She was a very old friend of mine," I said.

"Well, I never! My daughter's husband Ted used to
help her out sometimes, looking after her bit of land
and seeing to the animals when she was away."

"Ted? Not Ted Hood? Leonora often used to speak
of him!"

"Fancy that!" Mrs. Freeman handed me a cup of
very strong tea and an enormous slice of coffee

sponge. "It's a small world, that's what I always say.
Tragic, the way she died. Tragic."

"Yes, it was."

"Poisoned water, they say. Whatever next!"

"Well, I don't know about *poisoned*," I said. "Polluted, anyway. Something in the stream, apparently."

"That's rubbish," Mrs. Freeman said briskly, handing Thea an even larger piece of cake. "Our Ted said,
when we first heard, there was never anything wrong
with that water. He's drunk it often enough when he's
been working up there. And then there's those Bamfildes, they drink from the same stream and there's
nothing wrong with them. At least nothing that the
water could have caused! Nasty family, really unpleasant to poor Miss Staveley. Said they wanted to
divert the stream to water their fields. A lot of nonsense, that was!"

"Really?" I said. "I wondered about that. I was up
there a little while ago, and I couldn't see any fields
that they might need to irrigate."

"Exactly!" Mrs. Freeman said triumphantly. "Nothing to do with their farming at all. What they wanted
was to run it through their land to flush out their sep-
tic tank."

"No! But they couldn't do that. It would pollute the
stream . . ."

"Exactly."

"But that would be against the law."

"Not if they weren't found out," Mrs. Freeman said

vigorously. "Mind you, to be fair, I don't think they actually got around to doing it."

"Well, no, when I was up there I couldn't see anywhere where the stream had been diverted."

"Still," she said, pouring herself a cup of tea, "it just goes to show, doesn't it?"

I murmured my agreement through a mouthful of cake.

"Then, of course," Mrs. Freeman went on, "there was all that trouble about this new Leisure Center, whatever *that* may be. The whole place is up in arms about it, I can tell you. Well, I suppose there are one or two who think they may make something out of it, get jobs there and so on, that Trevor Barker, for one. But Esme—that's my daughter—said they're not going to want the likes of Trevor Barker at a swish place like they're planning to build up at the Manor!"

"I know Leonora was very against the whole thing," I said.

"Oh, there's been a great deal of feeling about it. Lots of big houses and estates around there. Of course people used to have houses there for the hunting, now it's just townees who want a place in the country. But *they* don't want a lot of people and cars all over the place. Anyway"—she paused for breath momentarily as she cut herself a piece of sponge—"my Esme's on the parish council and they've had several meetings about it; and then there was a general meeting where everyone could come."

"Really?"

"Oh yes. They invited Mr. Staveley to come and put his point of view. So he went and that wife of his."

The note of disapproval in her voice, I noticed, seemed to indicate a general dislike of Trish. I caught Thea's eye and she smiled.

"So when was this meeting?" I asked.

"Um, let me see now. It would have been on the Tuesday—no, I tell a lie, it was the Wednesday. Wednesday the twenty-third, it was. They'd been going to rearrange it because they wanted that Mr. Walters to be there—he's very well off and knows a lot of people who might have been able to help—but he had to be in London that week, and they couldn't have it the following week because the vicar—he's the chairman—he had to go up to Buxton that week because he'd promised to do a locum for somebody. So, where was I?"

"The meeting."

"Oh yes. Well, Mr. Staveley got up and said his piece—you know, about it being good for the village and so on. And *she* went on about how the facilities, as she called them, would be open to everyone. I mean! As if the people around there would want to go to those gymnasiums and have all that massage and health stuff! A lot of nonsense, if you ask me. Anyway, there was a lot of argy-bargy, and in the end the vicar said that there'd have to be a public enquiry and we all know what *that* means. It's all a case of who you know, isn't it, like the Council. That's why Esme says they want Mr. Walters to help them."

"I'm sure he'll do his best," I said, putting down my cup. "And now, if you don't mind, I think we'd like to have a look at the house."

"Goodness gracious! I was almost forgetting why you're here," Mrs. Freeman exclaimed. "Come along, I'll show you downstairs first. And I expect you'd like to see the garden. Jim, my husband, was a great gardener, but I'm afraid it's rather run wild since he died."

"Well," I said to Thea when we finally made our escape, "what do you think?"

"It's quite a nice house. Well built, good-sized rooms, and lovely large windows, so lots of light. And did you see, there's a good view of the sea from one of the upstairs windows. That would be nice—the one thing I'll miss about leaving the flat is the sea view."

"It's a good position, not too far from the village but well away from the main road. It seems in quite good condition, and once you'd got rid of that wallpaper, it could be really attractive."

"A definite possibility, I think. I'll get Michael to come and have a look at it. Though I hesitate to expose him to Mrs. Freeman's *torrent* of conversation."

"I know. Isn't it funny how much we enjoy Jane Austen's Miss Bates but shy away from the Mrs. Freemans of this world!"

Thea laughed. "It's the gloss of high art, I suppose. Mrs. Freeman is the raw material."

"Nevertheless," I said, "that sort of nonstop conversation has its uses. We now know about the Bamfilde's and the water supply and that the Staveley's were around on that particular day and that Harry Walters was away. And all without asking!"

Chapter Ten

I'd just finished baking some scones when Harry Walters arrived to collect Leonora's papers, so he came into the kitchen while I got them out of the oven.

"Those do smell good!" he said as he sat down at the kitchen table.

"I made them for the Red Cross coffee morning next week. I won't have time to do them nearer the day, so I'll put them in the freezer. But if you'd like one with your coffee . . ."

He accepted with enthusiasm, and I got a plate and knife and reached down for the butter dish and a jar of jam from the cupboard.

"Here," I said as I put a couple of scones on another plate, "help yourself." I spooned some jam onto a small dish. "It's bramble jelly, I hope you like it—but it's the one that's open."

"Oh, wonderful, it's my favorite. We never seem to have it now. Come to think of it, I don't think we have any sort of jam, and certainly not homemade scones."

"Doesn't your housekeeper do any baking?"

"Mrs. Stroud? She's more or less given up, poor

soul, since we're very rarely there for tea. So this *is* a treat!"

I made the coffee and sat down facing him across the table. He was still, I decided, a remarkably handsome man, tall and thin, with fine aquiline features and smooth hair whose silver still kept traces of its original fairness.

"How is Daphne? Is she at home or off on a case?"

"London, I'm afraid. Some Chambers' meetings, I believe, so she'll be staying up at the Clements Inn flat this week."

"It must get lonely for you," I said with just a hint of enquiry in my voice.

He smiled ruefully. "Well, that's the way it is when you're married to a successful professional woman. I'm beginning to understand how it must have been for Paula all those years ago, when I had to be away for a lot of the time."

"But Paula came with you when you actually had to live abroad."

"Yes, but—well, I suppose it's like me and the flat at Clements Inn. I don't really feel at home there, and when Daphne's with all her legal colleagues, I feel left out. I wonder if Paula felt like that, too?"

I laughed. "I think women are more adaptable than men, especially in situations like that. After countless generations of being dutiful wives, I imagine it came naturally. Mind you," I continued, absently taking a scone myself, "ours was the last generation—mine and Paula's—that felt that way. I can't see anyone of the present generation—Daphne, for instance—being like that."

"No," Harry said with feeling, "now the situations are reversed. I don't suppose this generation of young men see anything odd in being—what is it they call them?—house husbands. I do what I can, and I'm glad to say that I'm still useful to Daphne in many ways because of my contacts."

"Oh, I'm sure she is always grateful to you for all the support you give her," I said. "She owes you a lot."

"And I owe her too," he said. "You mustn't for a moment think I'm complaining! It's a very wonderful thing for someone my age to have a wife as young and successful and so full of energy as Daphne is. It's changed my life and I shall always be profoundly grateful to her. Take no notice of my moaning. It's just that I feel a bit down when she's away."

"Of course you do," I said. "And Leonora's papers will keep you well and truly occupied while she's away." I got up from the table. "Shall we go and look at them?"

I led the way into the garage and put on the light. Foss, who had been in the garden on some mysterious errand of his own, suddenly materialized and leapt onto one of the piles of boxes. "All these," I said, "are the books. The papers are mostly in that old filing cabinet over there."

Harry bent down and opened one of the drawers.

"There's quite a lot of stuff here," he said.

"Are you regretting your kind offer?"

"No, of course not." He rifled through some of the folders. "Have you looked at them at all?"

"I'm afraid not. It's all yours. Actually, I'd better see if I can find you something to put them all in. Do you think black plastic dustbin bags would do?"

"Good idea."

"Right. I'll go and get some—won't be a minute."

When I returned he was already leafing through one of the folders.

"Well, you're keen!" I said.

"There's some really fascinating stuff here. I've just found a letter from Scott Fitzgerald!"

"Good heavens!"

"It looks as if she met him when she was with Morgan Jackson."

"Well, little treasures like that buried in there should keep you on your toes."

We began to transfer the folders and loose papers from the cabinet to the plastic sacks.

"I gather there's going to be a public enquiry about that Leisure Center," I said.

"Yes, apparently. There was a meeting in the village a few weeks ago, but unfortunately I wasn't able to get there."

"Oh?"

"No, I was in London most of that week. I had to go to a dinner with Daphne at the Law Society."

"I think they—by which, of course, I mean the opposition—hope that you'll be able to pull some strings for them."

"I'm afraid my string-pulling powers are rather limited these days, but I'll certainly do my best for them—for Leonora's sake, if for nothing else."

"Good. As long as they know you're behind them. I really couldn't bear Vernon and Trish to triumph."

Harry laughed. "Well, we'll do our best."

"I hear the loathsome Matthew is home."

"Yes. I haven't run into him myself, but I believe he's been seen around the village. He is a nasty piece of work. I wonder if he's come back to see if there are any pickings from Leonora's will."

"No chance of that! He was never a favorite nephew, even when he was small and marginally more appealing than he is now. No—I think I can tell you, it must be more or less public knowledge by now—Leonora left the bulk of her estate to Marcus Bourne."

"Marcus Bourne?" Harry looked at me in bewilderment. "Who on earth is he? I've never heard of him."

"He's a young travel writer. He's also made a couple of documentary series about the more inaccessible bits of the Middle East."

"Good God."

"And you'd never heard Leonora speak of him?"

"No, not a word. How about you?"

"No. It's a complete mystery. Michael's firm are her solicitors, that's how I knew. But apparently they haven't been able to get in touch with him yet. Perhaps when they do, all will be revealed."

"Do let me know if you can. I'll be fascinated to

know." He tipped the remainder of the papers into the last of the plastic sacks and tied up the neck. "There, is that the lot?"

"Yes, it is. And thanks again for taking that particular burden from me. I don't know when I'm going to be able to start work on any sort of book, but it'll be wonderful to have them sorted. Then I can always send them to her college library (that's what I thought she'd want) for safe keeping. They really *ought* to be somewhere safe if there are valuable things among them, like that letter from Scott Fitzgerald. Then I'll feel able to do the book as and when I can."

"Good idea. Well, I'll be off. Thanks for the coffee and those wonderful scones."

"Any time."

He put the sacks into the back of his Volvo estate and drove away. As I went back to the garage to lock up, Foss suddenly appeared from behind the pile of cardboard boxes and wound around my legs, as I made my way back to the house, wailing in a way not to be denied, a pressing need for food.

I met Rosemary in the town next morning when I was on my way to the bank.

"Come and have a coffee," she said.

"Oh, I can't. Really. I've got a million things to do."

"So have I, but let's anyway."

The Buttery was crowded. "Full of visitors," Rosemary said sourly. "I hate the summer. Oh, look, those people over there are just going. You grab the table and I'll get the coffees."

"Goodness, I'm tired," she said as she came back to the table. "I got us two slices of lemon cake to keep our strength up."

"What have you been doing to make you so tired," I asked, "more than usual?"

"I had to do this dinner party for one of Jack's clients and his wife. He's quite important so, of course, Harold and Marion had to be invited too."

Harold is the other senior partner in their accountancy firm, Marion is his wife.

"What sort of client?"

"American. Sam Klein. Oh, *he* was sweet—you know how nice Americans are when they're nice? Well, he was."

"But?"

"His wife, Claire. Oh, she was sweet too, but so thin and elegant and expensively dressed and *groomed* within an inch of her life—do you know, she said she goes for a manicure every single week!—and cultured. She made me feel like a great big fat ignorant peasant."

"Poor you."

"Marion was no help. She just sat there with her mouth open while Claire told us all about the latest theater openings, a fascinating exhibition at some new gallery in SoHo (that really confused Marion!), and the only *possible* restaurants on the Upper East side. Honestly, it was like taking a crash course with the *New Yorker*!"

I laughed. "I bet you more than held your own."

"Well, I did try to give the impression that Jack and

I led a highly social life in the grandest country houses, in the intervals of riding to hounds and entertaining the Lord Lieutenant, but I don't know if she was taken in."

"You do *know* the Lord Lieutenant."

"Oh, well, it's only poor old Johnny Carmichael, who was at Cambridge with Jack."

"Still, she wasn't to know that."

"True. No, what I wanted to tell you was this. Sam Klein was talking to Jack about various people on Wall Street, and he let drop the fact that the firm that Matthew Staveley was with has come a cropper, and, as far as I can gather, the ghastly Matthew is out on his ear."

"Really!"

"Yes, it was quite a small firm by American standards, but fairly important in its way. But what's interesting is that Matthew is being made the scapegoat for things that went wrong, so his name is mud in financial circles over there—no possibility of a job in America, so *that's* why he's come home."

"Fancy that!" I said with some satisfaction. "That'll take him down a peg or two! And, of course," I went on, "this means that he'd be keener than ever to get this Leisure Center thing up and running."

"That's what I thought. *And* from what Claire said, he would have been back here when poor Leonora died. So you can add him to your list of suspects."

"Right. It doesn't sound as if he was at that protest meeting. I'm sure Mrs. Freeman would have made some remark if he was—she's very scathing about all that family! Perhaps he was keeping a low profile." Rosemary raised her eyebrows in enquiry. "I don't expect he wants anyone to now why he's back here."

"Oh no, he wouldn't, would he?" Rosemary agreed. "And Vernon and Trish would want to keep it quiet too, after all the boasting they've done about their financial genius of a son."

"They certainly tried to give the impression that he was only over here for a visit that time when we saw them in Taunton."

"You mean," Rosemary asked, "they were trying to give him an alibi for when someone poisoned Leonora?"

"Well, if they are, that means they have to be the murderers, because, as far as the general public is aware, Leonora's death was a dreadful accident."

"Well, then!"

I shook my head. "It isn't as simple as that. As we've said, they may have all sorts of reasons for wanting people to think Matthew wasn't here when Leonora died. Anyway, it wouldn't stand up as an alibi. The police could easily check when he actually arrived back in England."

"I suppose so," Rosemary said regretfully. She looked at her watch. "Oh, Lord, I've got to go! I'm supposed to be taking Mother to the opticians in half an hour, and I haven't picked up the fish for her lunch yet."

When she had gone I sat for a while, thinking about

what we had discussed and wondering how on earth I was going to find out exactly what Vernon and Trish *and* Matthew had been doing on the day when someone put something in that stream. The problem seemed to be insoluble, so I decided that I'd just have to wait for something to turn up.

That evening there was a dreadful thunderstorm. The rain came down in torrents, and the lightning flashes seemed to be right overhead. I'm not very good in thunderstorms—I'm terrified that lightning is going to set fire to the thatch. Foss always seems completely imperturbable, but poor Tris gets very upset. As the thunder rolled menacingly Tris crouched under my chair, his head close up against my ankles while I ate my supper, whining pitifully, whereas Foss, behind the curtains, appeared to be enjoying the spectacle outside. Rather than put the television on I picked up a book and tried to read. But I couldn't concentrate, and after a while I gave up and went to bed. Both animals came with me: Tris for comfort in his misery and Foss because he wasn't going to be left out of any unusual and potentially beneficial situation. They both slept on my bed so, what with that and the noise outside, I spent a restless night and woke in the morning unrefreshed.

As I drew back the curtains, I saw with some dismay that the stream that flows along the edge of the field behind the house had overflowed its banks in the storm and, washing down across a corner of my garden, had left a trail of mud and debris behind as it made its way downhill to the ford at the bottom of the lane. Michael telephoned while I was having breakfast to see if everything was all right, and I told him about the stream.

"Well, tomorrow's Saturday, so I can come along then and clear it up for you."

"Are you sure? I would be grateful. There are some quite large branches that have been washed down as well as stones and things. Bring Thea and I'll give you both lunch."

"Fine. See you then."

As we stood watching Michael clearing up the mess left by the stream, Thea said to me, "Can you remember if there was any heavy rain just before Leonora got ill?"

"I'm not sure. Why?"

"I just thought that if there had been, then whatever it was that polluted the water might have been washed down from much farther upstream."

"It's possible. I can't really remember. I think it *was* quite wet around then because we were afraid the rain might spoil Anthea's garden fete. Though, of course, it *could* have been quite different weather up there on the moor. Still, it's a thought."

"So where does that stream come from?"

"I'm not entirely sure. Up past the Bamfilde's it's all open moor, as you know. I don't know where it actually rises. Let's go and get out the Ordinance Survey map."

Having put out Foss, who likes to assist in these

matters, we spread out the map and tried to trace the origins of Leonora's stream.

"It seems to go back to *here*," I said, pointing to a spot some miles from the cottage. "Look, it goes under the road at this bridge here and seems to start in that combe, what's it called? Hawkcombe Water."

"I don't think I know that bit of the moor. Do you?"

"Yes, I drive over it when I go to see my friend Bridget at Hawkridge. And, as far as I remember, there are sheep on that bit of the moor."

"So that could have been the answer—a dead sheep, or just the droppings."

"I don't know. Here's Michael, let's see what he thinks."

Michael was very doubtful. "I'm all for exploring every avenue," he said, "but, honestly, it's a very long way from the cottage, and we didn't have the sort of flash storm that would have carried water from up there down that far and that fast."

"Oh, well, it was just a thought," Thea said.

"Well, as Michael said, we must consider every possibility," I said. "But I really do think we can rule out natural causes. I'm more and more convinced that there are too many people who wanted Leonora dead for it to have been an accident."

"Ma's quite determined to have something to investigate," Michael said. "Far be it for us to stand in her way."

"Go and wash your hands," I said severely, "then I'll dish up lunch."

Chapter Eleven

Time went on and what with knitting small garments and fussing over Thea (who bore it all with exemplary patience) as well as my usual activities, thoughts of Leonora's death and the reasons for it faded gradually into the background. It was only when Michael telephoned me one morning that it was abruptly brought to the forefront of my mind again.

"Guess what?" he said. "Marcus Bourne has surfaced."

"Really?"

"Yes, he's been in touch with his agent at last, and he's coming to see us some time next week."

"Where was he?"

"Wales."

"Wales!"

"I know. There we were imagining him on the road to Samarkand or somewhere equally exotic, and all the time he's been in Borth in North Wales."

"How extraordinary! What on earth was he doing there?"

"Don't know. I didn't ask and he didn't say."

"Oh, well, I dare say it'll transpire. So will *you* see him?"

"Yes. I'm in charge of Leonora's affairs, so I'll be dealing with him."

"Nice that he's actually come here and not just doing it all by letter."

"Yes. A bit odd really. Anyway, I thought you'd like to know."

I thought a lot about Marcus Bourne in the next few days. Trying to remember exactly what he looked like, I was annoyed with myself for not having videoed his television program. All I had was the impression of a rather intense, self-confident young man. I was wondering how I could manage to meet him when Michael telephoned again.

"Do you fancy dinner with us on Wednesday? Marcus Bourne is coming."

"Good heavens! How did that come about?"

"He rang me to say that he was going to be staying in Taviscombe for a couple of days and was there anyone he could see who'd known Leonora. So, of course, I thought of you,. Thea thought it might be more relaxed for everyone if we had dinner here."

"Brilliant!"

"I thought you'd be pleased. I know you've been dying of curiosity."

I had wanted to get to the flat early before Marcus Bourne arrived, to have a word with Michael and Thea, but Tris chose not to come in for the night when I called him. He lurked behind bushes in the garden and then rushed away just when I'd almost got a hand to him—a game that all cats play, especially when their owners are frantic to get out to keep an appointment. I finally managed to grab him, but when I got him safely into the house, to show his displeasure, he bit me sharply on the shin. The bite drew blood, so I had to deal with that as well as finding another pair of un-laddered tights. By the time I arrived I was out of breath, slightly disheveled and totally lacking in the composure that I had intended to bring to the situation.

"So sorry I'm late, Thea," I said as I took my coat off in the hall and thrust a bottle of Merlot into her hand. "That wretched cat!"

"Foss?"

"It's a long story. You don't want to know."

Marcus Bourne was sitting in a chair by the window and got up as I came into the room. "Mrs. Malory, your son has been telling me that you knew Leonora Staveley well."

"Oh yes, practically from childhood—mine, not hers!"

He smiled, a pleasant easy smile I had seen him give on television to some Papuan chief or some Kaza-khstan nomad's child.

"You were a close friend, then?"

"Oh yes. I loved Leonora and I miss her dreadfully. Oh, please, do sit down."

He resumed his seat by the window, and I sat in the

chair beside him. Michael brought me a gin and tonic and topped up Marcus Bourne's whiskey.

"Was she a friend of yours?" I asked. "Well, of course she must have been—I mean—well, it's just that she never mentioned you."

He took a sip of his drink and said slowly, "No, she was not a friend and I never met her."

I stared at him in bewilderment. "But I don't understand. Then why . . . ?"

"Why did she make me her heir?"

"Well, yes."

"I was her grandson."

There was complete silence in the room while we all assimilated this astonishing piece of news. Finally, since obviously someone had to say something, I said, "We never knew. No one did. She never told us."

He smiled, a different sort of smile, wry and ironic. "No, I don't suppose she did." There was silence again, then he continued, "She was very young when my mother was born, just at the beginning of her career. A baby would have been an—an inconvenience. And, at that time, the fact that she had an illegitimate baby might have finished her career before it had begun. So she had the child adopted."

Thea asked gently, "What about the father?"

Again, the wry smile. " 'Father unknown'—that's what the adoption papers said."

"You never knew?" I asked.

"No. My mother was never told and I had no way of finding out. I had my theories, of course."

I thought of Morgan Jackson and I could feel that Michael and Thea were thinking of him too.

Marcus Bourne looked around the room, apparently satisfied with the sensation he had caused. He certainly seemed to be a very self-confident young man, and one, I decided, who liked to be in control. I asked the question that was obviously expected of me.

"And what was that?"

"Well, it's no secret that she had an affair with Morgan Jackson when she was young."

"True. So you think he was your grandfather?"

"It seems very likely."

"But from what I've read about him, he'd have been delighted to have acknowledged any child he'd fathered—it would have contributed to the image."

"I think my mother was born after he died."

"Yes, I suppose that's possible. Leonora was with him up to the end. She left America when he died, came back to England, and then went out to Africa."

"What was your mother's name?" Thea asked.

"Gladys. That was the name she was baptized with by the people who adopted her. Gladys Jones."

"That sounds Welsh," I said. "Were they Welsh?"

He gave a short laugh. "Oh, yes. Very Welsh. Stereotyped Welsh, you might say. Hill farmers who adopted her because they wanted another pair of hands on the farm. Who lived by the chapel and listened to the minister, who said that the child was a child of sin who must be watched most strictly so that she didn't follow the path of sin herself. Can you imagine what that sort of upbringing did to a sensitive child?"

We were all silent following this outburst, then I said, "But she married. She got away from them."

"Oh, yes, she got away from them. They married her off to their nephew, a man twenty years older than herself, who needed a housekeeper—a servant to look after him and his two children when his first wife died."

"How terrible!" Thea said softly.

"And he was your father?" I asked.

"No. After five years of misery she ran away. A film crew was doing some location shots in the valley and—well, she was still a very pretty woman, even though she'd been worn down by all those years of wretchedness and, thank God, she still had enough spirit left to make a break for it. She went off with one of the cameramen, my father, Jeff Bourne. Her husband wouldn't divorce her, of course, so they couldn't get married, but I'm glad to say she had a few years of happiness. She died when I was ten."

"I'm so sorry," I said. "So your father brought you up."

"Not really. He was away most of the time, working. I lived with his sister and her husband. They were all right, but I found I wasn't cut out for suburban family life. As soon as I was old enough, I took off, worked my way around the world."

"It's extraordinary," I said. "The parallels between your life and Leonora's—the unhappy childhood, wanting to get away, traveling to remote places. Amazing!"

"No!" His voice rang out sharply. "I'm not like her!"

We looked at him in surprise.

"I couldn't abandon a child, just go off and leave it to a life of misery!"

"But she had no idea . . ." I began.

"Well, she should have! She should have made it her business to find out what sort of people . . ."

He stopped suddenly and it was as if a shutter had come down over his face, leaving it a polite mask. "I'm sorry," he said smoothly. "That was unforgivable of me—but you did ask."

Thea got to her feet. "I think the food is ready, if you'd like to come through," she said.

All through dinner (roast lamb, roast potatoes and new peas and a summer pudding—Thea was playing it safe) we all talked of other things. Marcus Bourne was most amusing about his travels. I felt he was putting on a show and that it was something he did whenever he wanted to control a situation.

When we were back in the sitting room with our coffee, Michael said, "Forgive me if I bring the subject up again, but how did you discover that Leonora was your grandmother?"

Marcus Bourne seemed to take a deep breath.

"Well, now. I suppose it started when I was in Nigeria, making a program about the Yoruba. They're very hot on kinship out there, you know, and they began to ask me about my family—and were amazed that I only knew about my immediate parents and hadn't bothered to find out more about my remoter antecedents. 'How can you know who you are,' they used to ask, 'when you do not know where you came from?' So I began to wonder and then, when I was back in England, I started to make enquiries. It's much easier nowadays, of course, and it had been a straightforward adoption."

"Had you heard of Leonora?" I asked curiously. "I mean, she hasn't done much recently, she isn't exactly a household name anymore."

"Strangely enough, one of my directors had worked with her on a program a while back. He gave me her address and I wrote to her."

"You wanted to get in touch?" I asked.

"Not at first. At first I was so angry—even angrier when I discovered that she had been famous and had led a rich and exciting life, while my poor mother . . ." He broke off for a moment, then, recovering himself, he continued. "No, at first, as I say, I couldn't bring myself to have anything to do with her. I loved my mother, you see, and I didn't see how I could ever forgive what had been done to her."

"Yes," I said, "I think I can understand that. But what changed your mind?"

He gave me a brief smile. "For a long time I've wanted to do this program on South America, all the myths and mysteries—lost cities, hidden gold, Colonel Fawcett, the lot. It would be a big project, take a lot of setting up. The BBC was interested, they'd buy it but weren't prepared to fund it. Neither was Channel Four, so I somehow had to raise the money myself to make the program. Well, sponsors are hard to find nowadays. There are so many expeditions to explore this and that, all looking for funding. The universities are out now and commercial sponsors will only contribute small amounts, useful but not enough for what I had in mind. So then I thought of Leonora Staveley. I reckoned that even if she couldn't raise all the money herself, she might know enough influential people to provide the rest."

"So you got in touch?" Michael asked.

He nodded. "It seemed to me that she owed me something. I wrote to her, explaining who I was. I played it casually at first, I didn't mention the program, just told her about my mother and myself. I didn't want to scare her off."

"How did she react?"

"Cautiously, asking for more details. That was fair enough, I could have been anybody. I sent her a copy of one of my books . . ."

"Ah yes," I said. "I saw it. It was beside her bed, just before she died."

"Oh." He seemed disconcerted by this. "Anyway, she asked me to go and see her, but I was due to do a book-signing tour in Canada, so I couldn't. But I put the idea of the expedition to her."

"And what did she say to that?" I asked.

"I think she was attracted to the idea, but she didn't

want to commit herself. I suppose it was rather a lot of money to be asked for out of the blue like that."

"I can imagine Leonora liking the idea, though," I said. "Just the sort of thing that would appeal to her. So then what happened?

"Then she died."

"And left you," Michael said, "the bulk of her estate."

"Yes."

"So now you'll be able to make your program," I said.

He hesitated for a moment and then said, "Yes, I suppose I can . . ."

"But?"

"But somehow I don't want to use her money to do it."

"But surely," Michael said, leaning forward to make his point, "that was what you wanted, why you approached her in the first place."

"It's difficult to explain. When I asked for the money I was angry with her, for what she'd done to my mother, to me even, bitter about all the wretchedness *we'd* suffered, when she and Morgan Jackson were rich and famous and leading glamorous lives. I wanted to take her money, if that was the only thing I could have from her. It seemed a way of paying her back for what she'd done. But then when she left me the money—just like that—there seemed no point in using it. Am I making sense at all?"

"Yes," I said, "I think so. Your anger was disarmed. You were left with nothing."

"Except the money," Michael said. "Surely it would be foolish not to use it."

"Perhaps I will," he said, "when I've got my head around the fact that she left me the money of her own free will, because she wanted to, not because I persuaded her to."

"You don't like a situation where you aren't in control?" I said.

He gave me a quick look.

"Possibly. I've always tried to be, I suppose I've always had to be."

We were all silent for a while, perhaps slightly overcome by the emotions generated by Marcus Bourne's story. Then the door, which had been ajar, was pushed open and Smoke came in. She looked around the room enquiringly, disconcerted to find it full of people. Then, with a little meow, she made straight for Marcus Bourne and jumped onto his lap, where she settled herself comfortably, curled her tail around her nose, as cats do, and promptly went to sleep.

"Oh, dear," Thea said, "I'm so sorry!" She half rose in her seat, as if to remove the cat.

"No, please. I love cats." He stroked the soft tabby fur gently. He turned to me. "Did Leonora have a cat?"

"Yes, a black cat called Charlie. She also had two dogs, two goats, several ducks, and a lot of hens."

"I wish now," he said, "that I had visited her; I'd

have liked to see where she lived. Would it be possible?"

I looked at Michael. "Well? What do you think?"

"Probate hasn't been granted yet, so technically Vernon can't claim possession. I still have the keys. Anyway, as the main beneficiary, you'll have to dispose of the contents. You know, of course, that Leonora left all her books and papers to my mother."

Marcus Bourne turned and looked at me.

"I think," I said, "she rather wanted me to do something with the papers and letters. I've written several biographies and edited a volume of letters, and I expect I will eventually."

"I see. A biography?"

"No, probably an annotated edition of the letters. There are many from distinguished literary figures and other well-known people that will be of general interest. With possibly a small selection of her journalism."

"I'd like to look at the letters sometime—that's if you don't mind."

"No, of course not. Harry Walters has them at the moment. He was an old friend of Leonora, and he very kindly offered to put them into some sort of order— they were pretty chaotic—so that I could work on them more easily. But I can get them back whenever you want to see them."

"That would be very kind." He stood up, and put Smoke gently down into the chair he had vacated. "And now, if you'll excuse me, I'll be going." He turned to Thea. "Thank you for a pleasant evening and a splendid dinner."

"Can I give you a lift?" I asked. "Where are you staying?"

"The Esplanade, I think it's called, the large hotel on the seafront. But, really, it's not far and I'd like to walk by the sea for a while. It's something I do whenever I can."

"I'm afraid," I said, "our muddy old Bristol Channel hardly qualifies as proper sea."

"There are waves and a shore." He turned to Michael. "I hope to be staying in Taviscombe for a little while, so if I could ring you sometime soon about going to the cottage?"

"Yes, of course, anytime. You have my number. I'll just show you out."

"Thank you. It's been a pleasure meeting you all."

When Michael came back into the room, Thea said, "Well! What a polite young man."

"Yes," I said thoughtfully, "I suppose so. But didn't you both feel that he was playing a part? All that about his mother and then himself, such a neat narrative, almost as if he'd rehearsed it. And the sudden outbursts of feeling, carefully controlled. I don't know why, but I can't help feeling that there's something behind it all."

"There's a lot of money," Michael said.

"Yes, and that's another thing," I went on, "all that bit about not feeling able to use the money. And is he *really* going to make a film about South America? I simply don't know what to believe!"

"Well," Thea said sensibly, "since he appears to be staying around for a while, we'll have an opportunity to have another look at him."

"You're quite right," I said, getting to my feet and collecting up the coffee cups. "Michael and I will do the washing up. You go to bed, you must be very tired after all that cooking—a super meal!—and you really ought to be getting a proper rest."

Chapter Twelve

A few days later, when I was in the supermarket, I saw they had a special offer on cat and dog food, so I thought I'd take a supply over to Pat Jennings for her animals. She really does run that place on a shoestring, and she's always grateful for any contribution. I loaded the box into the car and set off. It was quite a nice day, and after a while, the sun came out and I really enjoyed driving over the moor towards Dulverton. As I passed the track leading to Leonora's cottage, it seemed strange not to be turning down there.

I wondered what it would be like to go to the cottage with Marcus Bourne. He hadn't been in touch yet about fixing a date, and, somehow, I rather dreaded him doing it. I still wasn't sure what I felt about him. Was he really what he seemed, or had he been putting on an act in some way? I knew from his television programs that he was something of a "performer," could change his personality whenever it suited him. I wondered what he wanted from us. He had Leonora's money—was that all he wanted?

And why hadn't Leonora told me about him? I suddenly remembered what she had said about how nice it would be to have grandchildren—surely that would have been the moment. I felt hurt that she hadn't felt she could tell me, when I had thought we were so close. It couldn't be that she was ashamed to have had an illegitimate child—that wouldn't be like her at all. Perhaps she was ashamed of having had the child adopted and never trying to find out what had happened to her. But surely she'd have known that I wouldn't have judged her. I thought of her as a young girl, just finding her feet in the world, just starting out on her career, overwhelmed, as she must have been, by the death of the man who had played such a tremendous part in her life. And then to have found that she was pregnant, with no Morgan Jackson to turn to. Certainly she knew she couldn't have expected any help from her parents. Abortion was dangerous and difficult in those days, so it had to be adoption. And, having made the decision, I could see that, with the life she subsequently led, she would have put the whole thing out of her mind. I couldn't have done so. But, then, I wasn't Leonora.

The barking of the dogs in their pens at the animal refuge soon brought Pat out to let me in. She was delighted with the tins and invited me in for a cup of coffee. The old farmhouse was as free of creature comforts as Leonora's cottage had been. She even had a similar Victorian black leather sofa in an equal state of disrepair.

"Do sit down," she said. "I'll put the kettle on."

My sense of déjà vu was complete when, moving towards the armchair by the empty grate, I found a familiar black cat sitting there.

"Charlie?" I said enquiringly. "Pat, is this Charlie?"

"Yes, bless him, he was missing Leonora so much I bought him in here with me."

I picked up the cat, sat down in the chair, and settled him on my knee.

"That was nice."

"Leonora was a good friend," Pat said. "She helped me set up this place, and she was always there for me when things got difficult. I'm going to miss her."

"We all will," I said, "in various ways."

"She left me a small legacy, which will come in handy."

"Yes, Michael told me. She left me her books and papers."

"Ah," Pat said eagerly, "then there *will* be some sort of memoir. I was so afraid that when she died like that before she'd written it . . ."

"Written what?"

"Her memoirs. She was finally going to get down to it. I'd been trying to persuade her for years—such an exciting life, all the famous people she'd known!"

"And she definitely said she was working on it?"

"Oh yes. She said it was going to give some people quite a surprise."

"Really?"

"I don't think she'd started the actual *writing*," Pat said, "but I think she was planning it in her mind. I was saying to Mr. Walters just after the funeral what a loss it was—Leonora's dying before she'd had time to write it."

"Yes, well, Mr. Walters is sorting out some of the papers for me. As you can imagine, they were in no sort of order and there's some pretty important stuff there."

Pat laughed. "No, she wasn't what you'd call organized, was she? I often wonder how she got on abroad on all those assignments."

"Oh, she was very professional where her work was concerned," I said. I drank a little of my coffee, surreptitiously wiping the rim of the mug before I did so.

"Well, he'll be pleased—Mr. Walters, that is. He was very interested when we talked about it all."

"Did Leonora say *who* was going to get the surprise?"

"No, she didn't actually *say*, but I should think it would be that brother of hers. Wouldn't you, after the way he's behaved?"

"You think there might be some sort of scandal or something that Leonora knew about?"

"It wouldn't surprise me."

"Do you have any idea how he's getting on with planning permission for that Leisure Center?" I asked.

"There've been a lot of objections, as I expect you know, and meetings and suchlike. But I don't think anything's been settled. I did hear that Vernon Staveley's been around the village, telling people what a lot of jobs there'll be for everyone."

"I wouldn't think there'd be that many."

"Of course there won't!" Pat said scornfully. "Just a lot of flannel, trying to bribe people to stop their objections. They'll have to bring in all their fitness experts"—she pronounced the words with scorn—"and suchlike from outside. But then, there's always those who'll believe anything."

"So you think the Staveleys will get their way?"

"Sure to, in the end. Now that Leonora's gone and the cottage and the land is theirs. If it's turned down locally, they'll just take it to Exeter and I'm sure they can pull it off there."

I sighed. "So there's nothing we can do about it?"

"Not really. That's the way things are going in the countryside now. Golf courses, leisure centers, holiday cottages and tourists. Well, I'm glad I'm not young and growing up in this world. At least I've known it in the old days."

"I suppose people are better off now," I said tentatively.

"Don't you believe it!" Pat said vehemently. "There's a lot of real poverty about in the country, but it's just not as visible as it is in the town. People are prouder too; they try to put a brave front on things."

"Yes, I expect you're right. Oh, well," I said, giving Charlie a final stroke and getting up and replacing him carefully in the armchair. "I'd better be off. It's been good seeing you."

"Come any time. And thanks for the tins—you know they'll be appreciated!"

As I left I saw Leonora's two old dogs, curled up asleep together in one of the pens. I was glad that they would have a comfortable old age, with someone who would give them not only food but love and attention. What more, I thought, could any of us ask for in *our* final years? Somehow I didn't feel like driving back across the moor, but took the valley road beside the river, where the trees met overhead so that one seemed to be traveling through an endless green tunnel, the dappled light alternately dazzling or dim. It's very beautiful and I remembered that, as a child, I was sure that fairyland was just such an enchanted place.

Marcus Bourne phoned Michael the next day, and he arranged for us all to go over to the cottage the following afternoon.

"It's just me," Michael said when he arrived to collect me. "Thea's not very good at car travel at the moment, poor love. I said we'd pick *him* up at the Esplanade."

When we got to the cottage, it looked even more dismal than when I'd last been there. Weeds had sprung up, making the garden look overgrown and neglected, the paint had already started to peel on the front door, and the old Land Rover, which was still standing at the side of the cottage, looked particularly decayed and desolate.

"It's a bit gloomy, isn't it?" Marcus Bourne said as Michael got out the keys.

"Oh, all empty places look gloomy," I said defensively. "When Leonora was here, it was full of life, with all the animals around and always someone coming and going."

The sitting room was dark, and I switched on the light, which somehow made things worse, showing up the dust and general air of neglect.

I said, "It looks very bare now, of course, with all the books gone."

He didn't reply but opened the door and looked into the kitchen. I was suddenly glad that I'd done the washing up that last day. Somehow I couldn't have borne it if he'd seen the squalor of the dirty dishes in the sink. He gave the kitchen a cursory glance and came back into the sitting room.

"Are there any photos?" he asked.

Michael indicated the dresser where a couple of framed photographs stood, pushed toward the back. One of them was of a tiny figure standing in front of one of the Great Pyramids at Luxor—only the eye of faith, though, could identify the figure as the young Leonora. The other was taken in more recent times and showed Leonora, her face partly hidden by the large silver cup she was holding up, at some county show.

"That was when she won first prize for her lurchers at the North Devon Show," I said.

"Lurchers?"

"A kind of dog—she used to breed them."

"I see." He looked at the photographs for a while, and then he said, "Are there any more?"

"There may be some upstairs," I said. "Try

Leonora's bedroom; it's the first room on the right at the top of the stairs."

When he had left the room, I said to Michael, "What do you think he *wants* here?"

Michael shrugged. "To get some sort of idea what sort of person Leonora was, I suppose."

I picked up the brass dish that still had some cigarette stubs in it and shook it absently. "There's nothing of her here now," I said. "There's more of Leonora in these cigarette ends than any of the objects around the house."

"Are there any photographs upstairs?" Michael asked.

"I didn't see any, not on view anyway, but she may have put them away. People do." There was a step on the stairs, and Marcus Bourne appeared with two photographs in his hand.

"I found these in a drawer," he said.

He laid them on the table and we all bent to look at them. One was a studio portrait of Morgan Jackson, probably taken to adorn a book jacket. It had been taken in his middle age, before he knew Leonora. It was signed with a flourish: "To my darling girl—Morgan."

The other was more informal, an enlarged snapshot. It showed Morgan Jackson, now white-haired, but still tall and upright with his arm around a young girl dressed, like him, in shorts and a bush shirt. They were standing on the deck of a large yacht and, although the picture was in black-and-white, you could somehow sense that the sea and the sky were blue and the breeze that blew the girl's hair across her face was gentle.

"Is that Leonora?" he asked at last.

I nodded. "Yes, that's her."

"She was very beautiful," he said. "Like my mother."

"I never knew her when she was that age, of course," I said. "But she was good-looking really right up to the end. Though with Leonora it wasn't the looks you noticed, it was her vitality and—well, charisma, I suppose you'd have to call it."

"That's what attracted Morgan Jackson, you think?"

"That and the beauty, a pretty formidable combination. After all, Morgan Jackson wasn't the only one."

"You mean she had a lot of lovers?" he asked.

"Not a *lot*," I said. "That makes her sound promiscuous, and she was never that. No, she led the sort of Bohemian life that was fairly prevalent in those days in the circle she moved in."

"I see."

"It must seem like history to you—so long ago."

"Yes, a bit."

He was silent for a moment, then he said, "Morgan Jackson—he had two sons, didn't he?"

"That's right. One was killed in the war, but the other's still alive, I think, in Florida or somewhere like that."

"Did they know about Leonora?"

"Oh yes, it was never a secret."

"But not about the baby?"

"No one knew about that."

There was another silence. Then, "Did he leave her anything?"

"Money you mean?"

"Yes, or a manuscript or anything like that?"

"Not that I know of. Leonora wouldn't have wanted anything from him—nothing material, that is. That wasn't her way. Well, there is a copy of one of his books inscribed to her. It was by her bedside at the end, with yours."

"I see. And where is it now?"

"As I think I told you, Leonora left me all her books and papers."

"Could I see it?"

"Of course."

"What will you do with it? It would fetch quite a bit of money, I should think."

I shook my head. "No, I'd never sell anything of Leonora's. I'm going to give the books, and the papers when I've done the biography, to her old college at Oxford."

"Ah yes." He nodded. "The correct academic thing to do."

I looked at him in surprise at this caustic comment, and he said hastily, "No offense!"

"No, of course not. Actually, I know she left you the money, but I wonder if there's anything you'd like to have, as a keepsake, something personal. I mean, obviously everything in the cottage belongs to you, but if you'd like any of the books . . ."

He gave me that warm smile, the smile that I didn't quite trust. "That's really nice of you," he said. "Really thoughtful. Sometime, perhaps, when you've had a chance to look through them."

Michael picked up the keys from the table where he'd laid them.

"Right, has everyone seen everything they want? Shall we get going? It's a bit cold and damp in here."

Marcus Bourne nodded. "Sure," he said, "that's fine. Thank you both very much." He picked up the photographs. "Can I take these? Is it all right?"

"As my mother said," Michael said, "everything in the cottage belongs to you, and of course you must have those."

On the way back, Marcus Bourne didn't speak again of Leonora but was mostly silent just occasionally commenting on the Exmoor ponies we saw ("very like the rough little Mongolian ponies in some ways— I suppose they're almost as ancient") or the beauty of the landscape. When we dropped him at his hotel, he thanked us again.

"It was very good of you both to go to so much trouble. I do appreciate it. As you can imagine, it's been a strange experience for me."

"Will you be leaving soon?" Michael asked. "If so we'll need a forwarding address. There are still some documents to be signed—unless you'd like us to do things through your agent?"

"No," he replied slowly. "I think I'll be staying on here for a while. I'll be in touch."

As he walked away I said to Michael, "There's something about that young man I really can't take to. I don't know what it is. One thing's for certain: however many similarities there are between him and Leonora in the pattern of their lives, there's nothing of *her* there at all. None of her warmth and generosity of spirit. In fact," I said, "I don't think Leonora would have liked him either."

Chapter Thirteen

"Are you feeling brave enough to face Mrs. Freeman again?" Thea asked. "Only Michael's been with me to see the house, and *he* likes it, but there's a couple of things I'd like to look at again before we make an offer, and I'd like you to have another look too and see what you think."

"I'd love to," I said. "Whenever you like."

It wasn't a very nice day when we set out, overcast, and soon it started to rain.

"Still," I said, "it's best to see a house in all weathers. You both like it, though?"

"Oh yes. And it's not a bad price. We should get a decent amount for the flat, and we reckon that even when I give up work we can manage the mortgage."

"So you think you'll make an offer, then?"

"Yes. I just want to see about the side entrance—I didn't look very carefully at it last time—to see if we can make it safe. And I think we'll need a new bath and loo. I must check that."

"If you can escape Mrs. Freeman's chatter!"

"Oh, I forgot, she won't be there. When I phoned to

make an appointment, she said she had to visit her sister at the hospital today, but her daughter will be there."

Esme Hood had inherited not only her mother's cheerful manner, but also her inclination to chat.

"Ted sends his regards," she said. "I told him you were coming to see Mother's house, and he said specially to send his regards."

"That was kind of him," I said. "I remember how good he was to Miss Staveley. She always said how marvelous he was with the animals."

"Oh, Ted's dotty about animals," Mrs. Hood said with a laugh. "You should see him with our old dog, absolutely soppy he is with it."

"I know how much Miss Staveley appreciated all he did."

"Poor soul, dreadful to go like that!"

"Yes, it was a great shock to us all."

"Something wrong with the water they said in the village."

"Yes, E. coli."

"It just goes to show, though, doesn't it. You never know *what's* going on! We had those environmental people all over the village taking water samples everywhere. I said to Ted, I'm getting that bottled water for us and the kids—we've got two, a boy and a girl—I'm not going to risk anything happening to us. Mind you, we're on the mains in the village, but you never know, do you. I mean, goodness knows what science is going to come up with next—look at this BSE thing—though

we've always had a nice bit of beef for Sunday dinner,
I don't think you can beat it. Do you?"

She led the way, still talking through into the sitting
room. Thea declined her offer of a nice cup of coffee
and went off upstairs to look at the bathroom, while I
accepted and followed her out into the kitchen while
she made it.

"Only instant," she said as she poured the water
into the cups, "but between you and me, I can't really
tell the difference. Here you are, drink it while it's
hot."

I accepted the cup she gave me, and we sat cozily
down together at the kitchen table.

"Was there much talk in the village about Miss
Staveley's death?" I asked.

"Oh yes. Nine days' wonder, you might say. Well,
people thought she was a bit odd—she was what you
might call essentric, wasn't she?—but she was well
liked. Of course, we'd seen her on the telly too, not so
much now, but I can remember when she was, so people thought it was nice having someone famous like
that in the village."

"She was quite a character," I agreed. "And, as you
said, really quite famous in her day."

"Of course she lived in a bit of a muddle up there.
Ted used to say to me, 'Esme, you wouldn't believe
what sort of muddle Miss Staveley's cottage is in,' and
if a *man* notices, well! So in a way, we weren't surprised when she was taken to the hospital with food
poisoning. That's what they let on it was at first. I saw

Mr. Staveley—her brother that is—in the post office. I was just posting a letter to my sister Jean—do you remember her? She went out to Australia, she's got two lovely kiddies, a boy and a girl, like me! Anyway, when I saw Mr. Staveley, we got talking—we're both on the parish council, and I think he wanted to make up to me because of this planning thing—and *he* said his sister was in the hospital with food poisoning. But *then* when she died it all came out, about the water and everything."

"Have you spoken to Mr. Staveley about it since?" I asked tentatively.

"Oh yes. When the environment people did this report, we had a parish council meeting. Well, we thought we ought to know what was going on. Mr. Sargent, he's the vicar and our chairman, he read the report out to us. It was all double dutch to me, and to most of us if you ask me, all that scientific stuff about coliforms and suchlike."

"I know!"

"Well, I thought I'd better have a word with Mr. Staveley and see what it was all about. With Ted working up there. I mean, he'd have drunk the water there sometime, and I was worried he would get this coliform thing. But Mr. Staveley, he said he wouldn't unless he'd been working up there just before Miss Staveley was taken bad. Which he wasn't, because he'd promised to help Tom Thresher put up some fencing in his top field. Still, I said to Mr. Staveley, how can you be so sure? I mean, you can't take chances with that sort of thing, can you? And *he* said it was something to do with the tests they did on poor Miss Staveley in the hospital and then the water tests the environment people did. To be honest with you, Mrs. Malory, I didn't understand half of what he was saying, but he did seem pretty sure that if Ted hadn't been up there that week, then he'd be all right."

"That must have been a relief for you."

"Oh, it was. But I wondered afterward, how about Mr. Staveley himself, seeing as how *he* was up at Miss Staveley's cottage just before she was taken ill."

"Really?"

"Oh yes. You know the track leading to the cottage? Well, I was driving past to fetch Drew from school—he's my youngest and he's only four, so he comes home at dinnertime—that was on the Tuesday, I think, yes the Tuesday—before Miss Staveley was taken ill. Anyway, when I passed I saw his car. You couldn't mistake it, it's not a Land Rover, it's one of those great big American-looking things. It was parked up at the beginning of the track. There wasn't any sign of him, so I suppose he must have walked up to the cottage, though I can't think why. And it was still there when I drove back, and that was quite awhile after because, Miss Sylvester, that's Drew's teacher, wanted to have a word with me about him not taking sweets to school—well, I agree with her really, but it's difficult, isn't it, with kids, you can't turn out their pockets every morning, now, can you? So he must have been there quite awhile, so I wondered if he'd had a cup of tea or anything with his sister. Still, he's seemed all right since then, so I suppose it must have been okay."

I was about to question her more closely when Thea appeared in the doorway and asked me if I'd go with her to look at the side gate and the garden, and by the time we'd looked at a few other things the moment had passed.

"So what do you think?" Thea asked as we were driving home.

"Mm?"

"About the house. Do you think it will be suitable?"

"Oh, yes. It's a lovely situation, and the house is very well built and pleasant."

"Sheila, you're not concentrating. What is it?"

"Oh, I am really, and I *do* think the house will be perfect when you've done it up. It's just . . ."

"Yes?"

"Well, when you were upstairs looking at things, Esme Hood was telling me that she saw Vernon Staveley's car parked at the top of Leonora's track just a few days before she died."

"Well?"

"Why would he have called on her then? He hardly ever did. Towards the end they communicated almost entirely by letter."

"Perhaps he was just passing and had something important to tell her."

"Leonora never mentioned it to me."

"Well, if I remember, she wasn't really in a condition then to say much about anything."

"No, I suppose not," I said doubtfully. "But she was so obsessed about him and his schemes I'd have thought she'd have said something. Still, you're probably right." I thought for a moment. "But what if he wasn't actually *calling* on Leonora?"

"What do you mean?"

"Why didn't he drive right up to the cottage; he always did when he used to call."

"It's a pretty rough track; perhaps he didn't want to take his car down there if it was muddy or churned up."

"It was perfectly dry that week. Anyway, it's a great big hefty four-wheel drive, the track wouldn't bother it."

Thea carefully overtook a slow-moving tractor and a trailer precariously loaded with bags of silage.

"So what do you think, then?" she asked.

"There's a path leading from the top of the track that goes up into the wood where Leonora's stream is," I said. "Perhaps he'd gone up there."

"To put something in the water, you mean?"

"He could have."

"Leaving his recognizable car in full view of the road?"

"It's not a busy road," I said, "and he may have thought that no one would notice it."

Thea laughed. "Oh, come on, Sheila," she said, "this is the countryside. You know how, whatever you're doing, *someone* will notice."

"That's true. But while *we* know it, Vernon's not enough of a country person to have thought of that."

"Even if he did put something deadly in the stream—what sort of something, by the way?—there's no way you'll be able to prove it, short of a signed confession."

"No, I suppose not. Unless," I said, brightening up, "someone spotted him doing it. As you said, in the country there's always someone around noticing things!"

Later that evening, Thea rang and said that she'd discussed it with Michael, and they'd decided to make an offer for the house.

"Splendid," I said. "I'm so glad. I thought it had a good atmosphere, a proper family house. I think you'll both be happy there."

"It's the nicest one we've seen. And, anyway, I'd like to get everything settled and moved in before the baby arrives!"

"Goodness, yes, you'll have your hands full then."

"I told Michael what you've heard about Vernon Staveley being up at Leonora's that time, and *he* said perhaps Vernon had papers for her to sign."

"There speaks the lawyer," I said, "but I still think it was a bit fishy, and I'd like to think about it a bit more."

But the more I thought about it that evening and all the following day, the less I was able to come to any sort of satisfactory conclusion, either about Vernon Staveley's behavior or, indeed, about any of the inexplicable factors concerning Leonora's death. By the evening, I decided that I must put the whole thing out of my mind and get on with a bit of work. Cautiously I switched on my computer ("Ma," Michael had said, "you mustn't be *afraid* of it—! It's perfectly simple") and waited for it to present me with the familiar images. Instead a bloodred oblong appeared on the screen saying PLEASE CHECK SIGNAL CABLE. Before I could even react to this unexpected apparition, it disappeared and the normal things came onto the screen. But I was so disconcerted that I must have pressed the wrong key somewhere because my tool bar vanished, and, however much I tried, I couldn't get it back. In despair I phoned Michael.

"I'm so sorry to disturb you," I said, "but I've lost my tool bar."

"You've lost what?"

"My tool bar, on the computer."

Michael sighed. "*Now* what have you done?"

"Nothing," I said defensively. "Well, nothing that I can explain. It just vanished. And I can't get it back. I wouldn't mind, but I can't print out anything without it."

"Right. Switch on. And I'll talk you through it."

"Oh, dear," I said helplessly, remembering how on previous occasions I'd had to rush from the phone in one room to the computer in another with less than satisfactory results. "Couldn't you just tell me and I'll write it down?"

"Oh, all right. Now click on Start and get Set-
tings . . ."

When he had rung off and I'd tried and failed to
carry out his instructions, I sat down in front of the fire
with a gin and tonic. Like any dramatic conflict with
my computer, this one had left me feeling drained and
with a nascent headache. Attracted by an immobile
human being, Tris and Foss came in from the kitchen,
Tris flumping down heavily on my feet and Foss leaping onto my lap. He turned around several times, digging his claws into my knees as he did so, and settled
down for a good sleep as I reached for the television
remote control.

Rejecting a frenetic quiz show with "mammoth
prizes," some sort of gritty drama, shot mostly in
shadow, played by actors with unintelligible accents,
and a political interview that featured startling close-
ups of disagreeable-looking people mouthing plati-
tudes, I settled for a nature program. Since it took
place mostly in the desert and there were a lot of
camels, my thoughts drifted away to Marcus Bourne.

On the face of it a pleasant enough young man, but
there was *something* about him—I couldn't put my finger on it—I didn't feel I could trust, something I found
disagreeable. Fair enough, he'd had a difficult childhood, and he'd obviously adored his mother and
blamed Leonora for her unhappiness. Fair enough,
again. I just wished he'd been able to meet her and see
for himself what a remarkable person she was—it's so
difficult to try to explain one person to another. I sup-

pose that's what I felt I wanted to do with the memoir, using Leonora's own words, her writings and her letters, which brought her vividly back to life for me and would, I hoped, do the same for the rest of the world. And Marcus Bourne. Perhaps I could make him understand how it had been for her, so that he could forgive her.

He hadn't wanted to forgive her, though. He'd wanted a reason to dislike her, to use her for his own ends, to help finance his television program, making up to her, sending her the book with the fulsome but ambivalent inscription. I didn't like that. But now he said he didn't want to use her money, now that she'd made him her heir and the money was his. That's what he'd said and I wondered how true that was. I wondered, indeed, how true anything he'd told us was.

How much had he hated Leonora? Enough to kill her? He'd been in Wales—or so he said—not so far away. From his travels he'd known all about water supplies and what would pollute them. Perhaps Leonora had told him that he was her heir; I'd never known that, since she hadn't confided in me. Then he might have just thought that she owed him an inheritance and that he wasn't going to wait for her to die before he claimed it . . .

A sudden blast of music from the television awoke me to the fact that the nature program had ended and had been replaced by a young woman with a microphone, clad in shiny silver dungarees, jumping up and down in a sea of dry-ice while other young women, in less exotic garments, swayed back and forth behind her.

I turned off the set, put Foss carefully down on the sofa, and went off to make myself a cup of tea and lay the tray for the morning.

Chapter Fourteen

Nagged by the thoughts I'd had about Michael Bourne, the next morning I went into the garage to see if I could find the book by Morgan Jackson that I'd promised to sort out for him. I was looking helplessly at the mound of cardboard boxes, wondering where to start, when Foss, who had followed me into the garage, jumped up onto one of the boxes balanced rather precariously on top of the pile. His weight— he's getting rather chunky for a Siamese—brought it down, splitting it open in the process, so that the books inside spilled out onto the floor.

"Oh, Foss!" I exclaimed crossly. "Now look what you've done!"

He gave me a cold look, as though the whole thing was my fault, and stalked away, his tail, erect and swaying, indicating disapproval of no small order.

Resignedly I bent to pick up the fallen books. One of them, handsomely bound in leather, caught my eye and, idly curious, I opened it. It wasn't a book but a sort of diary—pages covered in Leonora's writing. Quickly putting the other volumes into what remained of the cardboard box, I took my find back into the house.

I sat down at the kitchen table and opened it. It wasn't a diary, exactly; that is, it didn't have daily entries, but seemed to be more a series of thoughts and descriptions, short paragraphs for the most part, as if she was using it to clarify her feelings. Some entries were dated, though, and it looked as if she had started it just after Morgan Jackson had died and she was back in England. There was quite a lot about her feelings after Jackson's death, the pain and desolation. It was quite clear how deeply she'd felt about him and how empty her life was without him—some entries were written in an intensity of despair that was painful to read about.

In London she'd met her old childhood friend Harry Walters again. She wrote about what a comfort he'd been and how he'd helped her through this black time, even, through influential friends, getting her the job on a prestigious newspaper, which was to start her off on her successful career. It was only after he had gone abroad with his company that Leonora had discovered she was pregnant and that the child was Harry's. The entries stopped there and the next pages were blank.

I put the book down thoughtfully. So Marcus Bourne's grandfather was not Morgan Jackson, after all. I thought he would be disappointed. There had been a note of excitement in his voice when he had spoken of the possibility. To be descended from a mere

businessman would not, I felt, have the same reso-
nance for him.

Then I suddenly thought of Harry Walters himself.
What was I to tell him? Obviously Leonora had never
told him that he had a child. She didn't want him to
know. Should I respect her confidence? But Harry still
had no children, and I knew that had always been a
matter of sorrow for him. And from what I knew of
Daphne, it seemed unlikely that *she* would want any.
Would it be fair of me to deny him the happiness of
knowing that at least he had a grandson? A grandson,
furthermore, who was on the spot, as it were, and
whom he could actually meet. These thoughts jostled
around in my head until I felt stupid, and I simply sat
there staring at the book in front of me. I was roused
from this state by the telephone. It was Thea.

"It's a bit short notice, Sheila, but would you very
much mind driving me to the clinic for my checkup? I
thought I could do it myself, but I feel a bit sick and
don't really want to drive."

"Of course I will. When's your appointment?"

"It's at eleven-thirty—in about an hour. Are you
sure you don't mind? I could cancel it . . ."

"Don't be silly! I'll be with you in about twenty
minutes." I thrust the book into a drawer in the dresser
and went upstairs to get ready.

Thea wasn't long in the clinic and felt much better
afterwards and able to face the idea of lunch.

"You must keep up your strength," I said.

"Yes, but nothing *too* heavy, just an omelette or something."

"So what did they say at the clinic?" I asked as we sat in an unusually quiet Buttery.

"Everything's fine. No problems. Well, except this wretched sickness. I should really be over it at this stage. Still, they said it probably won't be for much longer."

"Ginger biscuits," I said. "They're supposed to be very good—or actual ginger if you can bear it, or raspberry leaf tea. I'll get you some from the health shop."

Thea laughed. "You're spoiling me!"

"Nonsense, just trying to look after you."

I suddenly thought of the young Leonora, pregnant and alone, with no one to look after *her*. On an impulse I told Thea about the book and what I had found out.

"Good heavens!" she exclaimed. "So Morgan Jackson wasn't the father! Marcus Bourne *will* be disappointed! I'm sure he rather fancied himself as the descendant of someone as famous as that."

"You felt that, too?"

"Oh, yes." She paused and ate a small piece of omelette. "A young man on the make, don't you think?"

"Yes, I do. I'm so glad you feel the same. I thought perhaps I was prejudiced against him because of his attitude to Leonora."

"Michael thought so too. He told me about how Marcus Bourne behaved at the cottage."

"Yes. Not very—oh, I don't know—not thinking of

Leonora as a real person, just as a stepping stone to something else. Am I making sense?"

"Absolutely."

"At first I thought it was just a sort of irrational dislike—the Dr. Fell thing, you know—but the more I think about it, the more I feel that there is something unpleasant about him, and I feel sad for Leonora's sake."

"You are going to tell him? About Morgan Jackson, I mean. And about Harry Walters?"

"Well, I must tell him about Morgan Jackson, he's dead, so it doesn't matter. But I'm still not sure what I should do about Harry, and if I haven't told Harry then I can't tell Marcus Bourne. You see the problem?"

"Yes, I can see that there is one, but why can't you tell Harry Walters?"

I shrugged. "It's just this thing I have about respecting Leonora's wishes—or what I think might *be* her wishes. She obviously didn't want Harry to know about the baby."

"Yes. But that was then and this is now. It was all a long time ago, and the reasons she had for not telling him then don't really apply now, do they?"

I thought for a moment and then I said, "No, you're right. I wasn't thinking clearly. Of course I must tell Harry and then Marcus Bourne, and they must both make of the information what they will."

Thea laughed. "You sound as if you're washing your hands of the whole affair. I can't believe that!"

I smiled reluctantly. "No, well, perhaps not quite

that. Obviously I shall be curious to know how they resolve it all, but it's their affair. I'm merely the catalyst."

"So who will you tell first?"

"Oh, Harry, I think, don't you? Presumably Marcus Bourne will get in touch with him as soon as he knows, and Harry will need to be prepared."

But, as it happened, things turned out rather differently.

The following afternoon I was standing leaning on the seawall. I'd come down to feed the seagulls—or, to be precise, a particular seagull who only had one leg. I'd just thrown some bread for it and was pleased to see that it was more than holding its own, chasing off the other, two-legged birds that tried to intercept the food. It was a gray, overcast day and the sea, oily flat, and the sky seemed to merge into one, so that it was almost impossible to see where the horizon was. A melancholy sort of day and I stood for a while in mindless contemplation of the sea until voice behind me said:

"You look as if you are thinking deep thoughts, may I interrupt you?" It was Marcus Bourne.

"Good gracious! You startled me! No, I was just feeding the seagulls. You see that one over there, he's only got one leg, I worry about him, so I like to make sure he's all right."

"He looks pretty perky to me." He looked at me curiously. "You come down here specially for that?"

"Yes," I said defensively. "Yes, I know it sounds

silly. Michael always laughs at me for being so stupid about animals . . ."

"No," he said slowly, "it's not stupid to care for another living creature. Especially an animal. I greatly prefer animals to people, though I would have thought you, with what is obviously a loving family, might not feel the same."

"I think it's something you're born with. You can't really help it. My friend Anthea thinks I'm mad to allow my animals—I have a cat and a dog—to rule my life. But I love them, probably as much as—or more—than she loves some of her relations, and I want them to be happy!"

"I certainly felt closer to the ponies and the camels who traveled with me than I ever did about *my* relations. Except my mother, of course." He leaned his hands on the seawall. "That, incidentally, is why I was in Wales," he said. "I wanted to see the place where she was brought up, and try to experience what *she* had experienced."

"And did you?"

"No, of course I didn't. It was all different. Oh, I found the farm—that hadn't changed all that much— but all around it was touristy and, well, different."

"Life goes on."

"For some people."

We were both silent for a moment, then I said impulsively, "I have some rather unexpected news for you."

He looked at me enquiringly. "Oh?"

"It's about your grandfather."

"Morgan Jackson? What is it?"

"Just that he wasn't—your grandfather, I mean."

"What!"

I leaned my hands on the seawall. "I'd better explain," I said.

"Yes."

"I found a sort of diary belonging to Leonora, and in it she wrote—this was some months after Morgan Jackson had died—that she was pregnant and that the father was Harry Walters."

"Harry Walters?"

"He was an old friend who, well, tried to comfort her when she was so upset after Morgan Jackson died."

I turned and looked at him. He was standing absolutely still, almost as if he had been frozen into immobility, and his face was completely blank so that I couldn't tell what his emotions might be.

"I'm sorry," I said. "I'm afraid this must have been something of a shock to you."

He remained silent for what seemed like ages, then he said, "Are you sure? There's no possible doubt about this?"

"No, no doubt."

"I see."

He seemed to be holding in his feelings with a great effort, and I wished very much that he would say something, let go, release this tension that was building up in him, but I didn't know what to say, so I too remained silent.

The original seagulls, once the bread was finished, had long since gone, but others, seeing people standing by the seawall, swooped in to see if we had anything for them, whirling over our heads. As if awakened back to life by their hoarse, insistent cries, he turned to look at them and then turned to me.

"This Harry Walters—did he know about my mother?"

"No, I'm sure he didn't. I don't believe Leonora would have wanted him to know."

"Is he still alive?"

"Oh, yes. He was a few years younger than Leonora."

"So he doesn't know about me?"

"No, I haven't told him yet. I've only just discovered the diary."

"I see."

He was silent again, and again I remained silent too.

"This alters everything," he said at last.

"Well . . ." I began, but he interrupted me.

"The film I was going to make—it wasn't going to be about South America, I was going to make a film about them—Leonora and Morgan Jackson. You see," he went on with growing urgency, "you see how important it would have been. There's been so much written about Morgan Jackson. Everyone agrees he's the seminal figure in the literature of his period, so many films and stuff, but this would have been about *my* grandfather, full of entirely new material! It would have been a sensation—it would have made my name!"

He stopped suddenly and looked at me. I nodded.

"Yes, I can see . . ."

"And now," he burst out bitterly, "it's all been for nothing, all a waste."

"Did Leonora know that that was what you were planning to do?"

He hesitated for a moment. "No," he said. "I was still pitching her the South American thing. She was keen on that. But this was all by letter—I wanted to tell her about the Morgan Jackson thing face-to-face. I was going to visit her."

"Did she know that?"

"About the visit? No, I hadn't got around to it. I wanted to take things a bit at a time, take it cautiously. You know."

"So you never discussed Morgan Jackson with her."

"No."

"So why did you think that he was your grandfather?"

He shrugged. "I just got the dates wrong. I knew when Jackson died and when my mother was born, so I suppose I sort of assumed . . ." He laughed. "I assumed she'd been faithful to his memory—stupid stuff like that! How could I know she'd been sleeping around?"

"No," I said sharply. "Leonora wasn't like that. Harry was an old friend—it just happened."

"So why didn't she let him know she was pregnant?"

"By the time she knew for sure, he'd gone abroad, his first really important job. He was—still is—a biochemist, a very good one, and he'd just got a research appointment in America. There was no way she was going to jeopardize that for him."

"They could have married, or was he married already?"

"No, nothing like that, but Leonora obviously felt that it would have held him back, and she wouldn't have wanted that."

"And *she* didn't want to be held back herself, so she just abandoned the child."

"No, not abandoned. It's difficult to explain. It's all so different nowadays, things have changed so much, not, perhaps, always for the better. In those days, for a girl, having a child out of wedlock—you see how old-fashioned *that* sounds?—was a terrible thing. It could ruin your life forever. Some girls managed to have the child brought up within their own family, but that wasn't an option for Leonora. Her family would have disowned her."

"Oh, for heaven's sake, that's too melodramatic!"

"But that's how it was. I do wish I could make you understand. Soon single mothers may well be the norm, and there's all sorts of child care so that girls can go on working to support themselves and their children."

He didn't reply, so I went on. "Leonora was a sensitive person, I imagine it hurt her tremendously to give up the baby. Do try and think of that."

He shook his head. "I doubt if I'll ever be able to," he said. "It's all too painful for me. But, yes, as a sort of anthropologist, I suppose I've accepted that customs in other countries are different from ours."

"And," I said, "the past is another country."

He smiled reluctantly. "True."

"So what will you do now?"

He shook his head. "I don't know. All this has been a shock—all my plans ruined . . ." He looked out across the sea. A container ship just visible across the water near the Welsh coast seemed to hold his attention, then he said slowly, "I think I'll stay here for a while. Try and sort things out."

"You have Leonora's money," I said. "You can finance another film."

"Yes," he said absently. "I suppose I can."

Impulsively I put my hand on his arm. "Let me know if there's anything I can do for you," I said.

He smiled. "Thank you. That's very kind."

As I walked back to where I'd left the car, I looked back. He was still standing motionless, staring out across the Channel.

I felt depressed when I got back home. I made myself a cup of tea and fed the animals, but somehow I couldn't settle in to anything. I started to cut up a cauliflower for my supper, but it all seemed too much trouble. I laid down the vegetable knife and stood, looking out of the kitchen window, lost in thought.

Had I done wrong telling Marcus Bourne about his grandfather? Should I now tell Harry about his child and grandchild? Most of all, what would Leonora have wanted me to do? My head felt stupid—I couldn't think. I went back into the sitting room and picked up the phone. When Thea answered, I told her what had happened.

"So," I concluded, "I don't know if I've done the right thing by Marcus Bourne and whether I should tell Harry. It's all such a mess!"

"Of course you must tell Harry," Thea said firmly. "Especially now that you've told Marcus Bourne. For all sorts of reasons. I mean, Marcus may try to get in touch with him. Think how embarrassing that would be for everyone if Harry didn't know."

"Yes, of course, you're absolutely right," I said, encouraged by Thea's decisiveness. "That's what I'll do. It was just that I keep on wondering what Leonora would have wanted."

"One thing she *wouldn't* have wanted," Thea said, "would be for you to get yourself into a tizzy about it all!"

I laughed. "That's true. Thank you, Thea. I'd simply got myself into a muddle by not thinking straight."

"It's a tricky situation," Thea said. "Complicated. Not something that you'd have to decide about every day!"

"Thank goodness."

Then we talked of other things—how was Thea feeling, could she still not bear the smell of coffee, was working part-time being a success—until I gradually felt soothed and normal again.

"It's stupid," I said severely to Foss, who was up on the countertop supervising my preparation of a cheese sauce for the cauliflower, "to get all worked up about things. I must stop being woolly-minded and simply *do* things."

Foss, annoyed at the austere tone in my voice, jumped down off the countertop and stalked off into the hall, where he gave vent to his feelings by batting Tris, who happened to be coming towards the kitchen, sharply across the nose. The ensuing scuffle came as a relief as I gratefully gave my mind to sorting out my own minor domestic problem.

Chapter Fifteen

I really don't know *what* they put in muesli, especially that fiercely organic kind that you get in health food shops. I was dutifully plodding my way through a bowlful next morning when I bit on something hard, which turned out to be a large piece of grit or a small piece of stone. Whatever it was, it broke off the filling in one of my back teeth, leaving a painfully jagged edge. Resignedly I phoned my dentist, whose nice receptionist promised to "fit me in" at ten-thirty, and went off to get ready.

When I got there she was very apologetic.

"I'm so sorry, Mrs. Malory, but Mr. Browne's just rung through to say he's got a puncture, so he'll be a little late getting in. Do you mind waiting or will you come back?"

I said I'd wait and she went on, "I've managed to phone all his other patients with appointments this morning—all except Mr. Staveley. He said he'd wait, too. So if you'd just like to go through, I'll let you know as soon as Mr. Browne gets here."

In the waiting room I found Vernon Staveley listlessly leafing through a copy of *The Field*. He looked up as I came in.

"Oh, hello, Sheila. This is a confounded nuisance. There are a million things I should be doing, but I made the journey all the way into Taviscombe especially to see Browne. This new plate of mine is giving me hell, and I'm damned if I'm going all the way back without seeing him and getting it put right."

"How miserable for you," I said sympathetically. "Still, it isn't his fault if he's delayed. A puncture could happen to anybody."

Vernon looked unconvinced by this and muttered the word, "Inconvenient."

"How's Trish?" I asked.

"Oh, not too bad. She'd glad to have Matthew home, of course."

"Yes, I'm sure she is. When's he going back to New York?" I enquired maliciously.

"Oh—er—that hasn't been decided. He may stay over here for a while. He's been offered a very good opportunity with a firm of stockbrokers in London."

"Really?"

"Yes, well, we'll have to see."

There was a short silence, then he laid down *The Field* and said, "What's all this nonsense about Leonora leaving all her money to this television chap?"

"Oh, it's not nonsense," I said, "it's perfectly true." I deliberately didn't say more and waited for his inevitable question.

"But for God's sake, why him? Why leave it all to a stranger?"

I couldn't resist. "Oh, he isn't a stranger," I said sweetly. "He's her grandson."

"What!" Vernon swung around sharply to face me, knocking *The Field* to the ground. "What the devil do you mean? He can't be. Leonora wasn't married."

"No."

"You mean . . . ?"

"Her child, this young man's mother, was illegitimate. Yes. That's right."

"But I never knew . . ."

"She didn't want you to know."

I wasn't going to admit to Vernon Staveley that I hadn't known either.

"But when? Why didn't she say anything?"

"It was when she was in her twenties, when she was just starting out. She had the baby adopted."

"Adopted?" he echoed.

"Well," I said sharply, "she knew that she couldn't expect any help from her family."

"Well, she could hardly have expected . . ." He broke off when he saw the look on my face. "Things were different then," he muttered defensively.

He bent and picked up the magazine.

"So what's the story, then—about this young man?"

"Marcus," I said, "Marcus Bourne. As I said, he's the son of the daughter Leonora put up for adoption. He made contact with her shortly before she died."

"And she believed him?" Vernon expostulated.

"How do we know that he's who he says he is? He might be a con-man. Leonora left a considerable sum of money . . ."

"His documentation has been very thoroughly checked. Drayton and Green have acted for her for years, so naturally they went into all that very carefully."

"I see." He sat lost in thought for a while, then he asked, "And who was the father?"

I hesitated for a moment and then I replied, "Leonora never said."

"It's all pretty damned fishy, if you ask me."

"No, I think it's all quite straightforward."

"Bloody unfair, more like," he burst out. "*We're* Leonora's family, not some young chap she's never heard of before. She knew I was relying on anything she might leave to keep the Manor going. She knew how much the upkeep was."

"Ah, but she didn't approve of the Leisure Center scheme, did she?"

"You know how difficult and obstructive she could be! I did my best. I offered her perfectly good accommodation. After all, that cottage wasn't hers, it was only for her lifetime."

"Yes," I snapped back, really angry now. "For her lifetime. Until someone contrived to end her life!"

"What the devil do you mean by that?"

"I think someone poisoned her."

"What!"

I looked at him carefully. Was he genuinely surprised by what I'd just said, or was it bluster to hide his guilt?

"But she died of this water pollution thing."

"E. coli. Yes, but the source of the contamination could have been introduced into the stream by someone who wanted to harm her."

"That's rubbish!" He looked at me sharply. "Is that what these environmental people are saying?" he demanded.

"No," I admitted. "But it's perfectly possible all the same."

It seemed to me that he looked relieved at this. "So it's just some fairy tale *you've* cooked up?"

"Not a fairy tale," I said. "Not by any means. Not when you think of how some people have benefitted by Leonora's death."

"Now, look here . . ." he began angrily.

"Not just you," I said. "There's Marcus Bourne, remember, and there may be others that we don't know about. You had heard, hadn't you, that she was planning to write her memoirs. She covered a lot of ground in her career. There may be all sorts of people who would have wanted her out of the way."

"I suppose so," he said grudgingly. "But, Sheila," he leaned forward and gave me what he imagined was an ingratiating smile, "you can't imagine *I'd* ever do anything to hurt Leonora. She was my sister, damn it, and blood's thicker than water."

"But you wanted her out of her cottage."

"Yes, I admit that. It wasn't only because I needed

the cottage and the land—though that was part of it—but I really did worry about her. Living there like that, in those primitive conditions with all those disease-ridden animals."

"She was happy there. That was how she'd chosen to live."

"Yes, but honestly!" Here his tone became positively oleaginous. "You must agree that it was no place for someone her age. That's why I offered her a nice little house in Taviscombe, near the shops and the doctor if she was ill. Just before she died I went up there to make her see sense."

"She'd have hated it!"

"But she would have been safe there. At least she'd have had mains water!"

"Mains water isn't everything."

"Well," he replied tartly, "in Leonora's case it obviously was."

I didn't reply and there was an uneasy silence. Then Vernon said, "Have you told anyone else about this ridiculous theory of yours?"

"Yes," I said, "as a matter of fact I have."

"Who have you told?"

"Oh, various people."

"And did any of them believe you?"

"They felt there might be something in it."

"Oh, did they! Now, look here, Sheila, you'd better be very careful what you say about people, or you might find yourself in court!"

"Is that a threat?"

"No, a warning." He paused and then said in a more conciliatory tone, "Look, I know how fond you were of Leonora, but that's no reason to go around accusing people of killing her."

"I haven't accused anyone," I said. "It's just that I feel I owe it to Leonora to get at the truth."

He looked as if he was about to say something else, but just then the receptionist put her head around the door and called him in. As he went out he turned and said, "Just remember what I said, Sheila."

After Vernon had gone I tried to work out what I thought about him. Did he have anything to do with Leonora's death? He'd certainly *seemed* genuinely surprised at what I'd said, and his hostile attitude was probably that of someone who is being accused of something he hadn't done. But still . . . I was still wrestling with the problem while Mr. Browne was drilling out the old filling ("Have a rinse away") and putting in the new one, and, even when I was on my way home, I still couldn't make up my mind if he was guilty or not.

I stopped the car by the harbor wall, my usual place for thinking things out. There was no Marcus Bourne there today, but as I stood there gazing hopefully at the sea, as if it could provide me with an answer to my problem, a voice behind me said:

"*You're* miles away. Brooding about being a grandmother?" It was Roger Eliot.

"Roger! What on earth are you doing here on a Tuesday morning?"

"Playing truant, if you must know. I've just had one boring meeting, and I've got another in an hour's time and shut up in that office I felt I'd go mad if I didn't get a breath of fresh air!"

"Disgraceful!" I laughed. "No wonder crime stalks the streets of Taviscombe, if *that's* how the police go on!"

"So what about you?"

"Oh, just trying to think something out."

"A problem?"

"Yes. As a matter of fact it's about Leonora and that theory of mine."

"Now, why doesn't that surprise me? So, come on tell me what's on your mind. Bring me up to date on your investigation, Watson."

So I told him all about Marcus Bourne and gave him the gist of my conversation with Vernon Staveley that morning. "So you see, there are all sorts of reasons for people wanting her out of the way. Also," I added, "it seems that she'd told several people she was going to write her memoirs. That might have been a reason for someone to want her dead. Before she could do anything about it."

"Mm." Roger seemed to consider what I had told him, and I was silent, waiting for his response. When it came it was disappointing.

"Yes, I do see that you had reasonable grounds for suspicion—especially this Marcus Bourne turning up out of the blue like that—but the fact is, Sheila dear, you haven't an iota of proof; it's all supposition."

I sighed. "I know," I said, "it's absolutely maddening. I'm *sure* that somewhere there's one tiny bit of information, one little fact, that would connect someone definitely to the murder."

"You see," Roger said thoughtfully, "if there really was a murder, and if Leonora's death *was* caused by someone putting something—your dead sheep or whatever—in the water, it would be very difficult to prove."

"I know."

"So that, short of a confession from whoever did the deed—and I don't think there's much likelihood of *that*—I really don't see how you're ever going to catch this murderer of yours."

"You're right, of course. When you spell it out like that it does seem impossible."

"But?"

I smiled. "*But* I expect I'll go on ferreting away for a little while longer. It sounds absolutely ridiculous, but somehow I can *feel* Leonora urging me on! I can almost hear her voice telling me to get a move on and *do* something—just like she always used to when I was dithering about anything."

"And, of course, we all know you can't bear to leave a mystery unsolved. Well, carry on if you feel you must, but honestly, I think you're wasting your time."

"Probably. Oh, well. So how are Jilly and the children?"

"Fine. Delia's into Barbies now—she's got thirty-five of them."

"Good heavens! I'd no idea there *were* thirty-five. Where on earth does she keep them all?"

"You know those things with pockets in them for keeping shoes in, that hang on the back of the door? Well, she's got them in there. Each one has a name and number, and when she's going anywhere, she writes out little slips of paper with the numbers on and draws three numbers out of a hat and *that's* how she decides which Barbies to take with her when she goes visiting."

"I think that's brilliant. I do feel that such a practical girl has a great future!"

"Alex is into Lego in a big way, and, believe me, it's very painful treading on one of those ubiquitous little pieces of plastic if you haven't got your shoes on! Anyway, you have all that before you now. We were so pleased to hear about Thea."

"Yes. I'm longing for it. I always think that being a grandparent is the reward you have for having been a parent!"

Roger looked at his watch. "I must be going now. Keep up the good work, but don't expect too much."

After he had gone, I stood looking out to sea for a long time. He was right, of course. It would be almost impossible to prove any sort of foul play. But somehow that very fact made me even more determined to get to the bottom of the mystery. If no one else was going to do anything about it, then, more than ever, it was up to me. In my mind I could hear Leonora saying, "Come on, Sheila, get your finger out. That lot are no more use than a chocolate fireguard! You're a bright girl if you set your mind to it. You can work it out."

"Yes, of course I will," I said out loud. A passing dog walker looked at me curiously, and I hastily turned my head away. But somehow, now I was more determined than ever to carry on, for my own satisfaction as well as for Leonora's.

Chapter Sixteen

At the back of my mind was the feeling that I'd like to go once again to look at Leonora's stream, so the next day, although it was rather miserable, cloudy and overcast, I drove over the moor towards Dulverton. I left the car in a turnout a little way from where I could go into the wood and follow the stream. It was very quiet, there was no wind, no movement of the trees as I walked along the path until a pheasant, suddenly starting up just in front of me, made me jump with fright.

I stood quite still for a moment, looking at the stream. It had been a wet summer, and there was a fair amount of water rushing down over the stones and small rocks. I tried to work out in my head just how the murderer might have put the pollutant—whatever it was—into the stream, where it would be most effective, and, indeed, how long it would be before it took effect. But it was difficult, not knowing the scientific ins and outs of the affair. Why hadn't I paid more attention to science at school instead of sitting there in silent resentment at having to spend precious time on a subject I didn't like and wasn't any good at. The voice of my science mistress, Miss Udall, brisk and sardonic, echoed in my mind. "Sheila Prior, even if *you* find this a dreadful bore, others may wish to learn . . ."

Another voice, quite different, brought me back to the present.

"Here, what you doing there!"

I turned to find Jim Bamfilde coming up the path. As he approached he recognized me and said, "Oh, 'tis you. Where's that dog of yourn? He should be on a lead under proper control."

"Good morning, Mr. Bamfilde," I said in what I hoped was a friendly manner. "No, I haven't got my dog with me today."

He looked at me suspiciously. "What you doing here, then?"

"I thought I'd like to have another look at the stream," I said.

"What you want to do that for? Not still going on about that enviryment business, are you? I told you before, tidden naught but a lot of old nonsense. Nothing wrong with that water."

"Perhaps not, but I still wonder about the way Miss Staveley died. People keep saying that it was the way she lived—the animals and so forth—that harbored disease."

"That's daft. Nothing wrong with animals, we never caught nothing from them, and there've been animals around this yard ever since I can remember, and a long time before that."

"Oh, I agree."

"Lot of off-comers come to live here—they don't understand the country, don't like the noise and complain about the muck, mud on the road!" His face darkened, this was obviously a sore point. "Come here, " he continued scornfully, "buying up their country cottages—half the time they'm never here, and when they are they do naught but complain. Cas'n stand the sight of them. Won't have them on my land."

"No indeed."

"There was that young fellow a while back, set up his tent, bold as brass in my top field. I was'n having that. I sent Eric to see him off, but the bloody fool, he come back and says he couldn't do it. 'Why ever not?' I said. 'Because he's that fellow on the telly,' he says."

"What? What fellow?"

"Oh, 'tis some silly program he watches about foreign parts. Cas'n bide them myself. I likes the football and the news, but all the rest is rubbish. Eric, though, he's got these silly ideas—he likes these programs that tells you things. I got no patience wi' it. When he watches they, I goes out down the Royal Oak."

"So he, this young man, was camping on your land?"

"Aye. I was all against it, but Eric—well, he's meek and mild as a rule, but get an idea in his 'ead and there's no shiftin o' it. He said this fellow should stay, and I knowd t'was no use arguing."

"When was that? Before Miss Staveley died?"

He seemed surprised at my question but answered readily enough.

"Aye, couple of weeks before. He was there best part of a week, then he went away. Good riddance, says I."

"Did your brother find out what he was doing there?"

"What should he be doin' there—campers and they *ramblers*." He spat out the word with venom. "They just likes to go traipsing over other people's land. Says they've got a *right* to go where they want, leaving gates open and dropping they old plarstic bags. I'd shoot the lot of them if I had the chance."

"He didn't say if he was visiting anyone in the neighborhood?"

"Visiting?" Jim Bamfilde looked at me scornfully. "Who'd he be visiting 'round here? 'Tis only us and Miss Staveley, and for all she was a difficult woman, she wouldn't have had no truck with campers!"

"No, I suppose not."

He picked up the long-handled shovel he had laid down when we began to talk. "Well, I cas'n stand here all day gossiping. Got a ditch to clear."

He started to move away but stopped, turned, and said, "Don't you go on about that water—t'id'n naught to hurt. We don't want people messing about with thic stream. Besides," he threw over his shoulder as he went on up the path, "t'id'n going to bring her back."

I stood for a while taking in the implications of

what he had told me. So Marcus Bourne—for it was obviously him—had been here awhile before Leonora's death, and camping near the stream. He of all people, after his travels in primitive areas, would know about water supplies and what might contaminate them. Means, motive, and opportunity. Just like the detective books. If it was all quite innocent, why hadn't he told us that he'd been camping up here? Suddenly it seemed terribly important to know.

I drove straight to the Esplanade hotel and asked for him. The receptionist rang through to his room, but there was no answer.

"He must be out," she said. "Can I take a message?"

"No thanks," I answered automatically, my mind busy wondering where I could find him. I wandered out of the hotel and down to the seawall, and there— as I somehow knew he'd be—there he was.

"Hello," I said, "I've been looking for you."

He turned and said, "Well, here I am."

He looked at me enquiringly, but I was silent for a moment, not being sure how to approach what I now realized was going to be a delicate conversation. Obviously I couldn't come right out and say, "Did you kill your grandmother?"

"I've just been up by Leonora's cottage," I said, "and I walked up along the stream that flows past it."

"Yes?"

"Look, I'd better tell you straight out that I think your grandmother was murdered."

"What! But I thought it was some sort of food poisoning."

"Not food poisoning as such. E. coli—bacteria in the water supply. The water that comes from that stream."

"E. coli, yes I know about that. I've come across it quite a lot in the course of my travels."

"I thought you might have."

"So what? She died because of contaminated water. I'm afraid thousands of people in the third world do that, and no one says *they've* been murdered."

"But in this case several people would benefit from Leonora's death."

"Especially me?"

We stood facing each other. He looked angry.

"Why did you say that you'd never seen Leonora's cottage?" I asked. "Why did you let us think that you'd been in Wales all the time before she died?"

"What do you mean?"

"Why didn't you tell us that you'd been camping up there, near Leonora's?"

"Ah."

"Well?"

"How did you find out?"

"The farmer told me, the one whose land you camped on."

He smiled. "Oh, dear, the penalties of being on the television—instantly recognizable."

"You were unlucky," I said. "Jim Bamfilde wouldn't have known who you are—he thinks documentaries are daft—but his brother is a fan of yours."

"Oh, dear."

"So, are you going to tell me what you were doing there?"

"Apart from poisoning the water supply."

"Did you?"

"Oh, for God's sake! No, of course I didn't. What sort of person do you think I am?"

"Someone who is economical with the truth."

"I didn't lie."

"Why didn't you tell us? Why all the business of saying you wanted to see Leonora's cottage?"

"I wanted to go inside, I'd only ever seen the outside. You see, when I was up there, I was just, well, testing out the ground, doing a recce. That's what I do when I'm making my films. You have to tread carefully, you see, find out what the situation is, what the people are like, before you approach them properly. I suppose it's become second nature to me. I was just observing her, from a distance."

"I see."

"She was quite different from what I'd imagined, an old woman living alone with her animals. It shook me a bit. So I went back to Wales to think things out."

"And?"

"I wasn't sure what to do. I was confused. As I said, I never thought she'd be like that. I thought she'd be smart and slick—you know, foreign correspondent, been everywhere, done everything. That's how I imagined her when I wrote to pitch her my ideas. But then . . ."

"Then?"

"Then I saw her. She was out there feeding the fowl, an old woman, a peasant woman wearing a man's cap with a sack died around her waist. I really didn't know what to do. I still hated her for what she'd done to my mother, and I still needed her money to make my film, but seeing her there, well, she suddenly became a person, not the abstract idea I'd made in my mind."

"But you hated her," I said. "You needed her money—you've just said both those things. You knew from your experiences abroad about the dangers of contaminated water. You were camping right beside the source of that water supply. How can I believe that you didn't kill her, to avenge your mother and to inherit her money?"

"No!" he exclaimed violently, and a middle-aged man and a woman passing by looked at him curiously. He paused for a moment and then went on more quietly, "For one thing I had no idea that she was leaving me anything."

"I've only got your word for that."

"It's true. But, most important, I *couldn't* have killed her, I couldn't kill any human being." He shook his head as if to clear it. "When I've been abroad—the sort of places I go, you know—where life is very simple and raw, I've seen, in the most terrible circumstances of poverty, disease or disaster, just how precious human life is. For some people just the fact of being alive is all they've got. How could I quench that one spark, that one precious thing that we all have and should hold onto with all our being? How could I do that?" He looked at me earnestly. "Do you understand?"

"Yes," I said, "I understand. And I believe you."

We were silent for a while, both, I think a little shaken by what had been said.

Eventually I asked, "So will you make that South American film?"

He shook his head. "No," he said slowly. "I think I'm going to make a film about my grandmother and my mother—well, not about them exactly, but about their generations and how different things were then, such a very short time ago."

"I think that's a brilliant idea and I believe you'll do it very well."

"Thank you. Perhaps we can keep in touch. I may need your help."

"I'll be delighted. But, Marcus, there is one thing."

"Yes?"

"What about Harry Walters? Do you want to meet him?"

"You say you haven't told him about me yet?"

"That's right."

"Are you going to?"

"I feel I should. How do you feel about it?"

"It doesn't bother me either way. Now I know that Morgan Jackson wasn't my grandfather, I don't care who is."

"What about your Nigerians?" I asked. "The ones

who made you want to know who you are and where you came from."

He smiled. "They would understand."

I hesitated. "I think *he* would like to know. He's never had children. His first wife couldn't and his second wife doesn't want any—she's a successful barrister and much younger than him."

"Well, do what you think fit. I don't care. If he wants to get in touch, I don't mind."

"Well," I said uncertainly, "I'll see how it goes, then. Do try to come to terms with what's happened. You have *your* life to live, remember."

"I'll try to. You know, I've never been able to have any sort of proper relationship before. Perhaps now I can."

"I hope so." I held out my hand. "Good luck with the film and keep in touch."

He didn't shake my hand, but held it in both of his for a moment. "Thank you for everything," he said. "Thank you for trusting me and believing in me. I think you're the most important person I've ever meet in my life. And, Sheila, go on looking for whoever killed her. That's important too."

He turned abruptly and walked off along the seafront, among the groups of vacationers, until he was lost to my sight.

That evening I telephoned Thea to tell her what had happened.

"He really is a very odd sort of person," she said.

"You were rather doubtful about him, weren't you, so did you believe him?"

"Yes, I did. There was something, the way he spoke about things . . . I don't know. But I'm absolutely sure he had nothing to do with Leonora's death."

"So that's that, then."

"As far as Marcus Bourne is concerned, yes."

"But he was your prime suspect, wasn't he?"

"He was. But there's still Vernon Staveley." I told her about my conversation with him at the dentist's.

"I really don't know what to make of him," I said. "It could have just been righteous indignation, or he could have been hiding things. After all, he did more or less threaten me at the end."

"I don't think you'd call it a threat, exactly," Thea said cautiously. "Just a general warning, don't you think, not to interfere in his affairs."

"I suppose so. But with Marcus Bourne gone, he's really the only suspect I've got left now."

"What about the Bamfilde brothers?"

"No, now that I've talked to Jim Bamfilde, I'm pretty certain they didn't have anything to do with it."

"Well, there you are, then. Honestly, Sheila, I don't think you've anywhere left to go."

"No," I said with sudden resolution. "And we've all got much more important things to think about now, haven't we?"

"Well, I would be grateful if you'd come with me to the house. I want to measure up for the curtains and see what extra furniture we're going to need. Fortunately, I've got all the family stuff—this flat's always been a bit overcrowded with furniture—but there'll still be things that we need to buy."

"Not to mention all the nursery things," I said. "Or don't you want to do anything about all that until the baby is born? Some people don't."

"Oh, I think we must do the basics, don't you?"

"We'll have a day in Taunton doing all that," I said happily. "And, yes, I'd love to come and help you measure up. Actually, I've got quite a hoard of curtains in the ottoman. You must come and see if you'd like any of them, though I won't be offended if you don't want them!"

Thea laughed. "It is fun, isn't it? I'm beginning to get really excited, about the house and the baby and everything. Up till now it's all seemed a bit unreal— apart from the sickness!—as if it is all happening in a dream."

"You'll soon realize that it isn't a dream at two o'clock in the morning and no sleep for eighteen months!" I said. "But it's wonderful that you're so happy about everything."

But as I lay in bed that night, I couldn't help thinking once more about Leonora, and disconnected thoughts went squirreling around in my mind for what seemed like hours, until I finally drifted off into a restless kind of sleep.

Chapter Seventeen

"Actually," Thea said as we drove out to Porlock, "what would *really* be a help, would be if you held off Mrs. Freeman while I got on with the measuring. Do you mind?"

"No, of course not. And you're quite right, once she gets going we could be there all morning!"

So Thea politely declined Mrs. Freeman's offer of coffee and, giving me a grateful smile, went off with her tape measure in her hand.

"Well, now," Mrs. Freeman said, putting the kettle on, "what will you have? There's a piece of my shortbread or would you like to try an almond tart?"

"The shortbread would be lovely," I said.

"She probably can't take coffee now," Mrs. Freeman said, getting a tin down from the dresser and putting some shortbread on a plate. "My Esme was just the same when she was carrying their Drew."

I looked at her enquiringly.

"Oh, I know she isn't showing yet, but I can always tell! When's it due?"

"February," I said.

"Oh, that's nice. They'll have got well settled in by then. I'm really glad to think there'll be a baby here again, it's always been a real *family* house. I brought up Esme and our Jean here—she's in Australia now, did Esme tell you?—and we've all been very happy. Yes, it's a happy house. And you'll be pleased to know, nobody's ever died here."

"That's always nice to know," I said, slightly disconcerted by this information. "And how about you, when will you move into your new bungalow?"

"As soon as all this fal-lal with the papers is done. Esme's Ted—well, you know him, of course—he's decorated the kitchen for me. The rest's in very good order, so I can move in right away."

"How splendid."

I took a bite of the shortbread which was excellent.

"Is there any news about the Leisure Center?" I asked. "Have they got planning permission yet?"

"No, not yet. You can imagine how annoyed the Staveleys are about that! And do you know"—she leaned forward and lowered her voice—"it seems that Miss Staveley didn't leave her brother anything. Not a penny!"

"Yes, I had heard."

"But what was really weird, was she left it all to some person on the telly!"

"So I believe."

"Well, we were all flabbergasted, I can tell you! Esme says no one could believe it, the whole village was talking about it. It seemed very peculiar, though—

no one in the village ever clapped eyes on him. Still," she went on, "served them right, that brother and sister-in-law of hers, the way they treated that poor lady! Not a penny," she repeated with satisfaction.

She looked at me shrewdly. "Did you know him, then, this chap she left everything to?"

"I have met him, yes."

"And was he some sort of relation, then?"

"Yes, a very distant relation, they hadn't met for some years. But, as you say, Miss Staveley didn't want her brother to inherit."

"Well, I never!" She spooned some sugar into her coffee and stirred it vigorously. "He never came to visit her, then, this young chap. As I said, no one could ever remember seeing him—and you'd think they'd be bound to, with him on the telly."

"He was abroad a great deal," I said. "The programs he made were documentaries about distant parts of the world."

"Oh, I wouldn't have seen him, then," she said dismissively. "I like *Coronation Street* and *East Enders* and some of those cookery programs, but there's a lot of rubbish on now. And all that sex and violence in the programs now—it's so unnecessary, isn't it? Sometimes when I'm watching with Esme and Ted and our Rosie and little Drew, I don't know where to look, really I don't."

I murmured some sort of agreement and Mrs. Freeman went on, "No, I don't think that leisure place will ever be built now, in spite of all the Staveleys' efforts."

"Really?"

"Not now the people who were going to build it heard about the water being unsafe. Mr. Bazeley, he's the church warden and a regular busybody—not but what he did the right thing this time—he wrote and told them all about it, referred them to the Council and the environmental people, so they're certainly going to think twice!"

"That's very good news, though not for the Staveleys."

"Oh, she'll be sick as a cat if it doesn't go through. If you ask me, she's the one who's been pushing for it, right from the start. And that son of theirs when he got back from America. As a matter of fact, she and he had been up in London the day we had the meeting—only just got back in time. Went up there to see these development people. Well, I know, you see, because she and that Matthew went up by train the day before, and Fred Hobbs, he drives people to the station, and he heard them talking about it in the back of his car when he was driving them back. Full of themselves, they were, Fred told me, quite sure they'd 'pulled it off' as she said, laughing and joking. Well, they were laughing the other side of their faces when it came out about the water!"

"I do hope you're right and the thing won't go through."

"Mr. Walters doesn't think it will now. Esme saw him in the post office the other day, and he said it wasn't the sort of risk a company like that would take, and he's a businessman, so he should know about such things. Will you have another piece of shortbread?"

"No, thank you, it was delicious. Mine always comes out too hard, this has just the right sort of crumbliness."

"Perhaps you aren't beating up the butter enough. It makes all the difference . . ." While we were comparing recipes, Thea came back into the room.

"That's splendid," she said. "Our bedroom curtains will just fit the windows of the bedroom at the front."

"Now, I'm leaving the carpets," Mrs. Freeman said. "The one in the lounge has only been down a year, eighteen months at the most, and that one in the back bedroom, although it's been down for a couple of years, has had hardly any wear. Well, we used it as a spare room, you see, and we didn't have many visitors."

"The bedroom carpets will do for a bit," Thea said as we were driving home, "but I don't think I can live with that swirly pattern in the sitting room, even if it has only been down a year. It gives me vertigo just to look at it!"

"Will you leave the carpets at the flat?"

"Oh, I think so, don't you? They're all fitted and it's never satisfactory trying to put them anywhere else. Anyway, thanks for keeping Mrs. Freeman occupied! What did you talk about? Or rather what did *she* talk about?"

"Oh, this and that," I said vaguely. "She did say that

she doesn't think the Leisure Center will go ahead now. And she did say that Trish and horrible Matthew were in London the day before the meeting and only got back that evening."

"Aha! You've been pumping her! I might have guessed! I thought you were going to give up your 'investigation.' "

"It just came out," I said defensively, "in the course of conversation."

"Of course."

"Anyway, if those two were away at the crucial time, then it does seem to eliminate all the Staveleys—I really don't think Vernon has the intelligence or the guts to have done it—so that really does seem to be that."

I was just leaving the house to go and collect Thea to drive into Taunton to do some baby shopping, when the phone rang. I was already a bit late, and for a moment I thought I'd let it ring, but I never could ignore a phone, so I turned back reluctantly and picked it up. It was Harry Walters.

"Sheila, sorry I haven't been in touch for a while, but I've only just finished sorting out Leonora's papers."

"Oh, that's splendid. It must have been a mammoth task."

"It was rather, but fascinating. There's some very interesting stuff . . ."

"Harry, look, I'm in a bit of a rush, could you come

over one day soon and we'll talk about it then? There's something else I want to talk to you about, as well."

"Yes, of course. Sorry, I don't want to hold you up. Tell you what, you come to lunch here. Which day would suit you? Any day this week would be fine. Daphne's away, but Mrs. Stroud's not a bad cook, and I think she'd be glad to cook lunch for someone other than me!"

"Oh, that would be lovely. Would Thursday be all right?"

"Excellent. Shall we say about twelve o'clock? I'll look forward to it."

Thursday was a glorious summer day, bright sun and just a very gentle breeze. As I drove across the moor, the heather was fully out and the gorse and that especially delicate lemon-colored grass that I've never seen anywhere else. Harry's house was high up above Withypool. I imagine it had been built as a hunting lodge in the 1920s, since, along with the house, there was a range of outbuildings as well as some very handsome stables. I'd been there occasionally when Paula was alive, but I was taken aback by the changes that had been made to the interior since her death. The wood paneling in the drawing room had been painted white, the old mahogany furniture was gone and had been replaced by modern pieces in either cream or beige with long cream silk curtains at the windows. Light modern paintings (chosen, it seemed to me, more for their decorative qualities than their artistic merit) had replaced the oil paintings of English landscapes, and instead of the heavy chandelier there were spotlights and "interesting" lamps.

Harry saw me looking around the room and said, "Daphne wanted something a bit lighter. It *was* a bit dark, if you remember. She had this woman, a top designer I believe, in to do it over. What do you think?"

"It's very striking," I said, "and certainly much lighter." If he caught the sardonic tone in my voice, Harry chose to ignore it.

"Well, now, what will you have to drink?"

"Gin and tonic would be lovely."

"I think I've got most of the letters in chronological order now," Harry said as he handed me a glass, "and all the articles too. I wasn't sure, though, whether to group those according to subject or country, but there were quite a few on general topics, so in the end I thought chronological would be best."

"It sounds as if you've been very thorough."

He smiled. "I do love order. Paula used to laugh at me when I sorted my socks according to color! No, but seriously, I do enjoy sorting things out and it's given me so much pleasure to go through Leonora's papers. Some of the letters are quite important, I should think, from literary people—well, you'd know more about that side of things than I do—and politicians and suchlike. I've made a note of the dates, and I've tagged the letters themselves so that you can find them easily."

"That's brilliant. And no surprises? From what I gather, when she said she was actually going to get down to writing her memoirs, she implied that some people were going to get a shock."

Harry laughed. "Well, some of her letters—she kept copies of most of them you know—were pretty outspoken, and she never hesitated to give her opinion of people, however unfavorable, but that was her way. No, nothing shocking. Nothing to make it a best seller, I'm afraid."

"Oh, that's all right, then—no tiresome legal problems!"

"So do you think you'll be writing a biography, or what?"

"I'm hoping there'll be enough letters to make a complete volume, then I can simply slip in biographical sections to fill it out and explain the background. It's going to be a study of her professional life, I think, rather than her personal one."

"I think that's very sensible. Too many people nowadays seem to want every scrap of a person's life dragged out and put under a microscope, and the more sordid the better!"

I took a sip of my drink to brace myself for what I had to say.

"There is a special reason why I don't want to go into details of Leonora's personal life," I said.

He smiled. "Oh, you mean her love affairs. Yes, well, I agree that there's no point in raking all that up, though I think I'm probably the only one left alive now who might be affected. Still, perhaps people's children might be embarrassed . . ."

"In a way."

"Oh?"

"Not other people's children," I said.

He looked at me enquiringly. "What do you mean?"

"Oh, dear, it's difficult to know how to say this. I mean Leonora's grandson."

"What!"

"Marcus Bourne is Leonora's grandson. His mother was Leonora's daughter."

"What an extraordinary thing! Leonora never told me."

"Nor me."

"Who was the father? Morgan Jackson, I suppose."

"It wasn't Morgan Jackson. No, the reason Leonora didn't tell you about the baby is because you were the father."

He looked at me steadily for a moment and then said, "You're joking, of course."

I shook my head. "It's not something I would joke about. It's a fact."

"But if what you say is true, then surely she would have told *me*. I mean, it stands to reason, if I was the father."

"That's the reason she didn't tell you. She found out just as you'd got that research job in America—not a good time to be encumbered by a family."

"Yes, but . . ."

"And *she* was a very ambitious young woman. She didn't see herself sitting at home rocking a cradle."

"So what happened?"

"She had the baby adopted."

"And this lad Bourne is the grandchild?"

"That's right." I gave Harry a brief summary of Marcus's story. "He was very bitter to begin with. He was devoted to his mother and felt she'd had a rotten deal, but I think he understands things a little better now."

"That poor child—the girl—if only I'd known!"

"It was very sad. Though she did have a little happiness at the end."

Harry gulped down the last of his whiskey as if it was medicine. "If Leonora didn't tell you and the boy didn't know either, *how* do you know that I was the father of Leonora's child?"

"It was very odd. You know Leonora left me her books as well as all her papers? Well, I was just looking through them and I stumbled on this leatherbound book that wasn't a book at all, but a sort of diary—at least, not a diary as such. Just separate entries of things and events that she'd obviously felt important at the time."

"I see. Sheila, forgive me, can I get you another drink? I know *I* need one! This has all been a tremendous shock."

"Better not, I'm driving."

He poured himself another and came and sat down again. He seemed more composed and said, "I'd like to see this book, if I may."

"Of course."

"Does anyone else know about this? About the boy being my grandson?"

"Only Michael and Thea. Michael is Leonora's solicitor, and there was the inheritance . . ."

"Yes, yes, of course. It's just that I'd be grateful if you kept it to yourselves until I've had time to take it all in."

"I quite understand. As you say, it must have been a shock."

"What's he like, this boy? I think I may have seen one of his programs, but you know how it is, you never think of people on that little screen as being real three-dimensional people."

"I must confess I began by mistrusting him, but in the end I liked him very much. There's something of Leonora there."

"And you say you've told him that I'm his grandfather?"

"I had to, really, because of him thinking it was Morgan Jackson and the film and everything."

"Yes, I see. And how did he take it? Did he ask about me?"

I took a sip of my drink and decided to be honest.

"Actually, I think he was so disappointed to find out that it *wasn't* Morgan Jackson that he simply wasn't interested."

"Would he meet me, do you think?"

"Oh yes, I'm sure he would."

Harry sat for a moment staring into his glass. Then

he burst out, "Oh, it's all such a mess! If only I'd known! If only . . ."

"You mustn't blame yourself," I said. "It was Leonora's decision."

"What? Oh yes, I suppose it was, but everything would have been different if I'd *known!*" The door opened and the housekeeper came in to say that lunch was ready. Harry pulled himself together and said in almost his normal voice, "Thank you, Mrs. Stroud, we'll be in directly."

"I'm sorry, Harry," I said. "Perhaps I *shouldn't* have told you. Perhaps Leonora would rather you didn't know. But then," I added, "she must have known that I'd read that diary, so perhaps she did want you to know after all."

Chapter Eighteen

The dining room was done out in shades of dove gray with a blond wood table and high-backed chairs upholstered in gray and turquoise. There were those large square glass vases full of lilies and flower prints on the walls. It was all very beautiful, and I found myself wondering what had happened to Paula's enormous circular oak table and massive intricately carved sideboard. Gone to the salesroom, no doubt, and bought by some hotel keeper because they were certainly too big to fit into any ordinary house. Certainly the dining room was, as the drawing room had been, a great improvement stylistically and aesthetically on what it was in Paula's day, but I found myself resenting all these improvements in the sort of irrational way that led me to admit that it was simply because I couldn't stand Daphne and that nothing she ever did would appeal to me.

This time Harry didn't mention the changes to the decor—well, I suppose he had other things on his mind.

"Will you tell Daphne?" I asked when Mrs. Stroud had gone.

He didn't answer for a while and then he said, "Probably not. I don't know. To be honest, Sheila, I'll need to think how this might affect her."

"Affect her?"

"Her career, I mean. The slightest breath of any sort of irregularity—well, you know how things are in legal circles with everybody jockeying for position!"

"But surely anything like that couldn't *possibly* make any difference to Daphne!"

"You may be right, but I don't know if I should risk it."

"I wondered, actually, how Daphne herself might feel about it all."

"Ah yes, well, it was all a long time ago." He gave a short laugh. "Mind you, I don't believe she would care to have a stepgrandson not much younger than herself. She might think it looked a little ridiculous."

"Ridiculous?"

"Well, you know, odd."

"Yes," I said doubtfully, "I see." I ate a little of my salmon mayonnaise. Mrs. Stroud was a wonderful cook. The salmon was absolutely perfect, and on the side table there was a magnificent summer pudding, oozing juice, alongside a large bowl of clotted cream.

"And how do *you* feel," I asked, "about having a grandson?"

"It hasn't really sunk in yet," he said. "I just wish I'd known before. About the girl as well, Paula would have been . . . Well, you know how she longed for children. It's all such a muddle."

"Do you want to see him?"

"Again, I don't know. It depends on what I'm going to do about Daphne." He was silent for a moment and then he burst out, "Yes, of course I want to see him. How could I not? He's my grandson!"

I smiled. "Of course you do. I think you'll find him interesting—a very complicated young man."

"And he's going to make this film about Leonora's generation. He's using her money for that."

"Yes, I got the feeling that that was the only way he could justify taking it."

"A high-minded young man!"

"Not that exactly, just—well, complicated."

"Like Leonora." He spooned cream over his pudding. "I still can't get over her not telling me. I thought we were close. She was so dreadfully upset about Jackson, you know, almost suicidal. I was so grateful that she turned to me."

"From what she wrote in the diary, I'm sure she was deeply grateful."

"I thought at the time," he said sadly, "it was more than gratitude. I was so in love with her."

"Oh, I think she came to love you too," I said. "I'm sure she did."

"Love, but not 'in love.'" He smiled. "I suppose I knew that and was prepared to settle for anything as long as we were together."

"That's probably the other reason she didn't tell

you," I said. "As well as not wanting to put anything in the way of your career. She may have felt that a child might bind you together and perhaps she didn't want that. I'm sorry, was that a hurtful thing to say?"

"You're almost certainly right," Harry said. "I'd hoped there might be a future for us together. I was very young. Leonora was altogether more realistic; she knew that what we had was only something transient, something to get her through. When we met later on—those other times—we were both older and wiser. We knew that, although we'd always have that sort of attraction for each other, any sort of commitment would never had worked. I suppose I should be grateful to her."

"She must have been grateful to you," I said. "You more or less saved her life twice."

He laughed. "Oh, you know Leonora, couldn't bear to be beholden to anyone!"

"That's true. You know," I said sadly, "that's what really upset me, that last time I saw her, she seemed not only glad to see me, but actually *grateful* for the little things I did for her. I suppose I knew then that she wouldn't get better."

"Poor Leonora. But as we've all said, she couldn't have carried on living like that, and being anywhere else would have made her utterly miserable."

"You're right, of course," I said, "but it's always difficult to be sensible about someone you care for."

After lunch Harry said, "Let's go into the library, and I'll show you what I've done with the papers."

To my surprise, the library was more or less un-changed—I suppose because it was Harry's domain and Daphne couldn't be bothered to do anything with it. Her presence, though, was very definitely there. There was an easel by the window and on it a large and handsome painting of Daphne in her barrister's robes and wig. It was painted in the manner of an eighteenth-century portrait, with Daphne standing in front of a looped velvet curtain and holding a scroll in her hand. I half expected a Latin inscription. I felt the artist thought he was painting Shakespeare's Portia ("Oh, wise young judge") for he had found a nobility and graciousness in his sitter that I had never observed in real life.

"Oh, you're looking at Daphne's portrait." Harry came over and stood beside me. "I got Anstruther to do it—he's the best man for that sort of thing, don't you think?"

"It's very handsome," I said, "a magnificent picture."

"They want it for a retrospective of his works at the National Portrait Gallery," he said. "I wasn't sure if I wanted to lend it, but Daphne thought we should."

"Oh yes, I'm sure Daphne is right."

"Well, now, let me get out the notes I made."

We worked on the papers for about an hour, and I was impressed by the methodical way he had dealt with all the problems.

"And I do know from experience what a lot of work is involved," I said. "I really am very grateful."

"I enjoyed it. At my age it's nice to have a project to

work on. I'll just go and get some boxes for these, and we'll get them into your car."

As I was waiting for Harry to come back, the house-keeper came into the room.

"Mr. Walters said, would you like a cup of tea before you go?"

"Oh, no, than you, Mrs. Stroud, I'm fine. Especially after that really delicious lunch."

She looked pleased. "Well, I must say, Mrs. Malory, it's a real pleasure to have someone else to cook for. There's quite a bit of entertaining when Mrs. Walters is here, of course, but that's not very often nowadays, and when he's alone Mr. Walters doesn't really notice what he eats."

"No, I suppose men don't notice these things."

Apparently emboldened by this remark, Mrs. Stroud said confidentially, "It's a real shame the amount of time he spends alone. He goes to London quite a lot, but between ourselves, I don't think he really likes it up there. But when he's down here, there's not a lot for him to do—he's on the parish council, of course, and he used to putter about in that laboratory of his, but he hardly ever does that anymore."

"Laboratory?"

"Oh, he had the old tack rom fitted up as a laboratory. Said he wanted to keep up with things—that being his line in the old days, as I expect you know. But, as I say, he's even lost interest in that. So I was ever so pleased when he brought all those old papers back from you to sort out. It's kept him really interested, he's sat up quite late some nights going over them!"

"I'm glad he had something to occupy him," I said. "It's been a great help to me."

"This is such a big house for one person to rattle about in. It would be different if there were children and grandchildren."

"Yes, indeed."

"There now, I shouldn't be saying all these things, but with you being such an old friend of Mr. Walters . . ."

"Oh, yes, very old friends. And, of course, we both knew Miss Staveley."

"Poor soul! Not that *I* ever knew her, of course, except just to say good morning to in the shop. Kept herself to herself."

"She liked her own company."

"Mr. Walters used to go and see her sometimes. In fact, he went up there just about a week before she died."

"Really?"

"Yes, I thought when she went like that, how glad he must have been that he saw her that last time."

"Yes, I'm sure he was."

"He was in London all that next week, of course— some sort of legal thing they had to go to. But he phoned at the weekend to see if everything was all right, and I was able to tell him then that Miss Staveley had gone. He sounded quite upset, poor man."

"Yes, we were all very shocked."

The door opened and Harry came back into the room. "If you'd like to give me your keys, Sheila, I'll put the boxes in your trunk."

I said good-bye to Mrs. Stroud and went outside with him.

"Do let me give you a hand," I said, "some of these boxes are quite heavy."

"No, that's fine, I can manage. Now, won't you stay and have some tea with me? No? Well, you must come again soon. It's been so good to have your company."

"I've had a lovely day," I said, "and thank you again for all your work." As we shook hands, I added, "I do hope all the things I told you weren't too upsetting."

"No, my dear. It's just that you are leaving me with a lot to think about. Oh, by the way, if you *could* let me have a look at that diary of Leonora's . . ."

"Yes, of course you must see it. I'll get it out and you must come to tea with me and collect it."

"That would be splendid."

I got into the car, and as I drove away, I could see him, still a tall, upright figure, but somehow rather forlorn, standing looking after me as I went down the drive. I thought how well Harry had taken the news about Marcus Bourne. He'd been upset, naturally, and I think he'd been hurt that Leonora had kept him in the dark for all these years, but I felt that in the end he'd understood. I very much hoped that he *would* get in touch with Marcus, and that Daphne wouldn't spoil that relationship for him. Harry was the sort of person who should have had children, and if by this extraordinary quirk of Fate he was suddenly provided with a ready-made grandson, as it were, then I wanted him to enjoy it. There was also the fact that he was a very rich man and could do a lot to help Marcus. I began to weave a fantasy whereby Harry financed a proper film—a cinema film that might win an Oscar—for Marcus to direct.

A large flock of sheep, urged on by a man and a couple of dogs, coming towards me on the narrow moorland road made me slow down and concentrate on my driving. One of the dogs ran in front, neatly heading off any sheep that might wish to stray from their destined path, while the other rounded up the stragglers at the rear and those sheep who wanted to stop off for a quick bite of grass. The man simply walked behind, apparently content to let the animals do his work for him. Dogs, of course, work with human beings; cats, of course, work against them.

When I got in, it took me a long time to unload all the papers and put them back in the garage. It was heavy work, and when I had finished I was quite tired and didn't feel like looking for Leonora's diary. Instead I fed the animals, made myself a cheese omelette, and spent most of the evening dozing in front of the television.

The next morning it took me quite awhile to remember where I'd put the diary, but I eventually ran it to earth in the dresser drawer, where I'd put it that day when Thea had telephoned me. I opened it and idly flicked through the pages. To my surprise, I realized that there were more entries after the last one I had read. Leonora had left several pages blank and then started again. I sat down at the kitchen table and began to read.

The next entry, after the last one I had read before, was obviously several years later and was an account of her time as a hostage in one of the Gulf states. Although her style was quite prosaic, even understated, the description of the situation and the people involved was vivid and immediate. I could almost feel the heat and discomfort and the ever-present smell of fear. She ended up with her release, arranged by Harry Walters. ("Good old Harry to the rescue—what a tremendous fixer he has become!")

Again, a few pages were blank and then what really did seem to be the final entry. She was writing in Nigeria, sometime in the sixties, I think, though there wasn't a date. It was the description of a disaster at some sort of chemical plant that had caused the death of several hundred people. The international firm that was obviously responsible (bad conditions, faulty maintenance and safety regulations) was trying to hush up the whole affair, which would certainly have brought worldwide condemnation.

Negotiations were taking place to "persuade" the local authorities to publish a report saying that it was an unfortunate accident—"human error," "no blame can be attached . . ." and so forth. The chief negotiator for the company was their administrative director for the area—Harry Walters.

I sat back in my chair and looked at the handwritten entry in amazement—I couldn't believe what I had just read. Harry Walters, the Harry I knew and respected, engaged in this illegal sordid cover-up. Lying and bribing his company's way out of trouble when hundreds of innocent people were dead—it didn't seem possible. Then I began to wonder why Leonora, a probing investigative journalist if ever there was one, had never exposed the whole ghastly mess. I began to read on. Certainly Leonora's immediate instinct was to write the story. It was exactly the sort of thing she did well—factual, unemotional, utterly convincing. Then she had a meeting with Harry at the local hotel. What he said to her, what feelings she wrestled with over several days she did not say, but the next entry was the flat statement: "I cannot write this story." There was a space on the page and then the words, "And I don't believe I ever will." Underneath, written in a shaky hand and in different, unfaded ink, was the word "NEVER."

I pushed the diary away from me and put my head in my hands. For a while I simply couldn't take in what I'd been reading, but then I began to consider the implications for Leonora and for Harry. *Why* had she condoned the cover-up, made herself, in effect, an accessory to their crime? For I'm sure that must have been how she saw her part in the affair. She must, of course, have felt a great debt of gratitude to Harry for saving her life, but perhaps most of all because she knew that he was the father of her child. That must have been why, for this one time, she wasn't faithful to her own strict code of journalistic ethics. It would have been a hard decision, and one that would have influenced her attitude to her old friend and lover.

Now I came to think of it, although I knew that Leonora and Harry were old friends, I'd hardly ever seen them together when they were both back in the same part of the county. I suppose I'd assumed that Leonora had shared my own dislike of Daphne (indeed I'd often heard her speak disparagingly about her) and that she and Harry had drifted apart because of this. But now it was clear that she had been avoiding him. This wouldn't have been obvious to all her friends and neighbors, because for a considerable time Leonora saw virtually nobody. But the illusion had been preserved that the two were old—and dear—friends. Indeed Mrs. Stroud had, only yesterday, told me how pleased she was that Harry had gone up to see Leonora for what later proved to be the last time.

I sat up with a jerk. *Why* had Harry gone up to the cottage? If they hadn't been close for all that time, why would he go and see her then? My mind was in a whirl. Automatically I opened the door for Foss, who had been demanding to be let in; automatically I spooned cat food into a dish and put it on the floor for him.

"But it *can't* be!" I exclaimed out loud.

Foss raised his head from his dish, looked at me reproachfully, and then continued eating. If what I had read in the diary was true and Leonora held that secret, and if she was proposing to write her memoirs, then Harry Walters may well have thought he had a good reason to want her dead.

Chapter Nineteen

I tried to gather my thoughts into some semblance of order. Leonora knew something about Harry's past that, if it came out, would not only be discreditable to him but would, most probably, also affect Daphne's career. Leonora had let it be known that she was about to write her memoirs. This would make Harry very anxious indeed. However, Leonora had specifically stated in her diary that she would never publish that story. *But* Harry wasn't to know that.

Now then, after Leonora's death there had been an attempted break-in at the cottage. Was that Harry, trying to get in to steal Leonora's papers? He was certainly very keen to know what was going to happen to them. What I had taken to be the interest of an old friend may well have been something more sinister. He had accepted with alacrity my suggestion that he might sort out the papers, but he'd found nothing there. Even now, because I hadn't read the entries when I saw him, he didn't know that I knew about the secret. Perhaps I should keep it that way, at least for the moment.

The telephone rang and I looked at it with some misgiving, thinking, in the state I was in, that it might be Harry demanding to see the diary. When I finally got around to answering it, I found that it was Thea.

"Sheila, are you all right? You sound a bit strange."

"What? Oh, sorry, yes, I am a bit."

"What's the matter?"

"I can't really talk about it over the phone. Do you think you could possibly come over?"

"Well, actually, I was just ringing to see if you'd like to come here for coffee. I've got some patterns of material for curtains I'd like you to see."

"Oh yes," I said gratefully, "that would be splendid. I'll come over straightaway." I managed to pull myself together, more or less.

"Whatever's the matter, Sheila?" Thea asked as she led the way into the sitting room. "You sounded most peculiar on the phone."

"I've had a bit of a shock," I said. "It's about Harry Walters."

"Oh, dear, what's happened to him? Is he all right?"

I sat down and Thea poured me a cup of coffee.

"No, it's nothing like that. I mean he's all right, nothing's happened. Well, I suppose in a way it has."

Thea looked at me. "You're not making sense! Drink your coffee and calm down and tell me all about it from the beginning. Here, have a biscuit, it might help."

I took a sip of coffee and a bite of the chocolate digestive and told Thea all about the diary entries.

"Oh dear, I do see what you mean. It's a very strong motive. But, Sheila, was it really strong enough for him to *kill* Leonora, after all she'd been to him?"

"I think it probably was. That secret had been hanging over him for years; the thought must always have haunted him that one day it might come out."

"Yes, I can see that."

"And you must remember that he didn't know about the baby then. He didn't know that he was the father of Leonora's child."

"True."

"The thing is," I said, "even if he was prepared to ride out the media fuss about what he did *himself*, he'd be frantic about what it might do to Daphne's career."

"She'd probably divorce him! And he is absolutely crazy about her."

"Exactly."

We were both silent for a moment, then Thea said, "And you say that Mrs. Thingummy, the housekeeper, said he went up to see Leonora just before she died?"

"Yes," I said. "He could have poisoned the stream then."

"What with?"

"What do you mean? Oh, I see." I thought for a moment, then I said triumphantly, "The laboratory, of course!"

"What laboratory?"

"Harry has set up a small laboratory in one of the outbuildings. He used to be a biochemist, as you know." I broke off. "You see!" I exclaimed. "Biochemistry! He could perfectly well have made the culture or whatever it is of the E. coli things. No messing about with dead sheep or anything—so simple!"

"Good heavens!"

"That *must* be what happened, it all fits in!"

I leaned back on the sofa and finished my coffee.

"It certainly sounds quite plausible," Thea said.

"Of course it does. Means, motive, opportunity," I quoted.

Thea thought for a moment. "Not quite," she said. "Not opportunity."

"What do you mean? Of course . . ." I broke off. "Oh yes, I see."

"You said that the environmental people reckoned that the pollution must have occurred not more than three days before her death. Harry was in London all that week. He couldn't possibly have done it."

The excitement drained out of me. "No," I said disconsolately, "he couldn't have."

Thea refilled my coffee cup. "Perhaps it *was* an accident, after all," she said. "Well, natural causes, at any rate."

"Perhaps so. But then *why* did he go to see Leonora that last time, then?"

"It could have been about the planning permission for the Leisure Center, something quite simple like that. It doesn't have to be anything sinister. Besides, if he was going to do anything wrong, he wouldn't have told his housekeeper where he was going."

"I suppose not . . ."

"Anyway, I'm sure you wouldn't really want to think of Harry Walters as a murderer."

"No, of course not. And yet, it all seemed so . . . Oh, I don't know."

"It really isn't possible, Sheila."

"No, you're right. Come along, what about those curtain material samples?"

Harry rang me a few days later. After a little desultory chat he said, "Did you manage to find the diary, or whatever it is?"

For some reason I found I couldn't bring myself to let Harry see it. "Oh, I'm so sorry, I haven't had a chance to have a proper look for it yet. I can't seem to lay my hands on it. I *know* I put it away somewhere safe, but I can't for the life of me remember where! And I've been dreadfully busy this week—it's the Brunswick Lodge garden fete this Saturday, and, like a fool, I let myself in for organizing the catering and absolutely *everybody's* let me down, so I've been baking for days on end! But next week when I'm not so frantic, I really will have a good look for it."

Taken aback—as well he might be—by this torrent of misinformation, Harry said mildly, "There's no hurry, anytime will do. It's just that I'd rather like to see it . . ."

"Of *course* you do. It's only natural, after all." Then, as curiosity got the better of me, I asked, "Are you going to get in touch with Marcus Bourne ?"

He didn't reply at once, then he said, "I think so. I

think I must. How do I get in touch with him, have you got an address?"

"In the nature of things, he moves about a lot but his agent will always forward anything."

I gave him the agent's address and then asked, "And you won't tell Daphne?"

"No, I think not. I don't think I can face all the explanations. I'll arrange to meet him when Daphne's away on some trip or other. There are always," he added sadly, "a lot of them."

"Yes, that will probably be best."

"Well, I'd better let you get on."

"I'll be in touch soon."

I got the impression, as I put the receiver down, that he would have liked to talk longer, but my feelings about Harry were now so confused that I really didn't want to continue the conversation.

That night we had another thunderstorm, not such a bad one as before, but this time the electricity went off. Our electricity supply is completely capricious. Really bad weather—storms, wind, heavy snowfalls—frequently leaves it unscathed, but, as Rosemary once said sourly, just let a medium-sized bird alight on a wire then the whole thing goes off immediately.

Fortunately, since the situation is fairly common, I always have a good supply of candles and several oil lamps. Electricity only came to our part of the country relatively recently (just before the war, in fact) so my mother, ever provident, kept some of the oil lamps that used to be our only form of illumination. Mind you, one forgets just how dim the light of such lamps is after the brilliance of electric light, and I never like to light candles to supplement them because they have a fatal fascination for Foss, who has been known to poke at them experimentally with his paw. Since there was no television and I couldn't see comfortably to read, I decided to write off the rest of the evening, and once the thunder and lightning had ceased, I shut the animals away in the kitchen and went to bed.

When I woke up I was delighted to see that my clock radio was flashing and power had been restored. After breakfast I began the tiresome task of resetting all the clocks on the electrical things. I'd just got up from crouching in front of the video recorder when I stumbled and knocked one of the oil lamps off a small table. Fortunately the oil didn't spill all over the carpet, but the glass chimney broke into two pieces.

The only place I know (probably in the entire country) where you can still get an oil lamp chimney is Ellicombe's. They sell everything anyone living in the country could possibly want, from tractors to teaspoons, and they take up a large portion of a neighboring village about ten miles away. Going to Ellicombe's is always a treat, although you may come away with more than you bargained for—I have an enormous ball of binder twine (invaluable in the garden) from there that will last *me* for quite a while and probably Michael as well. And at every county show you can bet that the largest crowd will be gathered around their stand, which is a sort of unofficial meeting place for old friends to gather.

Driving past the serried rows of brightly colored agricultural implements, I went into the shop proper. Bypassing the stands of saucepans and crockery, wicker baskets, huge boxes of assorted nails, screws, and suchlike, I made my way through the clothing section (racks of Barbour jackets, waterproof trousers, farm overalls, boxes of tweed caps, and row upon row of Wellington boots of every possible variety, from the delicate green townie version with itsy buckles to enormous black ones suitable for digging ditches in the muckiest weather) to the single counter.

Behind the counter, a collect of signs for sale covered most of the hazards of the countryside warning one to beware of the dog, the bull, the electricity pylon, and much else. On the counter itself were leaflets for various agricultural products (fertilizers, pesticides, drenches for cattle) as well as those advertising for local events (olde tyme fetes, pig roasts, duck races). The man in front of me had a very complicated order that necessitated the solitary assistant wandering off into the considerable hinterland to search for various esoteric items, so I settled myself down for a long wait. This is all part of the ritual of buying anything at Ellicombe's, and you simply have to adjust your time scale to theirs. It's quite peaceful, really.

I was just considering the various merits of a collection dog show at Stogumber or a Young Farmers' Barb-Q with music by Jethro and the Sheep Rustlers, when my eye was caught by another leaflet, which I picked up and put into my shopping bag for more careful perusal later on.

When the assistant had carefully examined the two halves of the broken chimney I had brought with me and estimated the size, thickness, and general quality of the replacement I required (Ellicombe's assistants, as well as having no sense of time, are also well-known for the degree of meticulous service they provide—the one being consequent upon the other), he disappeared for a further fifteen minutes. Usually on such occasions I go off into a sort of mindless daze, but today, being anxious to get out and examine the leaflet more closely, I was unable to relax into that agreeable state and found myself actually feeling impatient at the wait.

When the assistant finally came back, I cut short his long dissertation on the peculiarities of various kinds of oil lamps ("You won't beat the old Aladdin—proper lamp that were"), paid for the chimney, and hurried out of the shop, leaving the young man looking puzzled and a little hurt. Back in the car I fished the leaflet out of my bag and began to read it.

"New Monosoluble M95 Water Soluble Film Features Faster Solubility and Packaging Uses," said the headline in large black print. "A new polyvinyl alcohol (PVA) water-soluble film now offers a broader range of packing possibilities for agricultural chemicals," it went on. "This formulation provides a slightly faster solubility rate than others previously available." There was a great deal of very technical stuff I couldn't understand, but one thing was now clear—Harry Walters *could* have put E. coli bacteria in the stream, enclosed in this water-soluble film, and it could have seeped into the water and done its deadly work while Harry was away in London with a perfect alibi.

I sat in the car park for some time while various thoughts chased themselves around and around in my mind. Finally I put the leaflet away and drove home. I still wasn't sure what to do with this new information now that I had it. Nor was I sure who, if anyone, I should tell. Perhaps I ought to talk to Roger—or Michael, or Thea. Perhaps I should confront Harry himself. I simply couldn't decide. Instead I did what I often do in moments of stress; I got out all ingredients and made a fruitcake. While I was preparing the fruit, washing and drying the currants, sultanas, and cherries, then coating the cherries in flour so that they wouldn't sink to the bottom, and while I was beating the eggs and sifting the flour and creaming the butter I deliberately made my mind a blank. I greased the cake tin and cut the parchment for the bottom and the sides, concentrating only on the matter at hand, enjoying the feeling of my wooden spoon moving through the mixture and its final disposition in the tin. Only when I had shut the oven door and set the timer did I allow myself to think about what I had found out. I made myself a cup of coffee and sat down at the kitchen table and really *thought* about it—about everything, the facts, the possibilities, the consequences—and I came to a decision.

When I had finished my coffee I phoned Harry and asked him to come over.

"Would tomorrow morning be all right?" he asked. "About ten-thirty?"

"That will be fine."

"Good. I'll look forward to it."

Fortunately I didn't see anyone for the rest of the day or the evening, so I didn't have to explain why I was so on edge and distrait. I got up extra early the following morning and did a thorough vacuuming and dusting. I put fresh flowers in the sitting room and laid out a tray with coffee cups and biscuits. As I put water in the percolator, I thought how odd it was to be making coffee for someone I was about to accuse of murdering one of my dearest friends.

Harry was punctual; almost exactly at ten-thirty the doorbell rang and almost reluctantly I went to answer it.

I showed Harry into the sitting room (no cozy chat at the kitchen table today) and gave him the leather-bound book that contained so many secrets.

"Have a look at it while I get the coffee," I said. I paused in the doorway. "There are several other entries that I hadn't read when I saw you last."

He looked at me enquiringly, but I closed the door behind me and went out into the kitchen. I stood leaning against the countertop by the window, watching the coffee bubbling up in the percolator. I wanted to give him time to read all the entries. Outside on the bird feeder a young woodpecker was hammering away energetically at the peanuts while the blue-tits regarded furiously from a safe distance this intruder in their midst. There was probably, I felt, some moral to be drawn from this, some parable to illustrate the menace of power, but I had to go and face a difficult situation and had no time to consider it now.

Tris, who had been in the garden, barked to be let in and followed me as I went back into the sitting room with the coffee.

"White, is it, with no sugar?" I handed him a cup, poured one for myself, and sat down while Tris settled himself at my feet. "Do help yourself to biscuits."

Harry looked up from the book. "You've read it, then?" he asked. "All of it?"

"Yes."

"I see."

He picked up his cup and stirred the coffee mechanically. "I can see how it must look to you," he said. "It was a long time ago, that episode in Nigeria, and it was an extremely difficult situation for me."

"How did you persuade Leonora not to write the story?"

"She knew it would ruin me. So I begged her, I really *begged* her—for the sake of our friendship, for what we had once been to each other, all that . . . But, to be honest, knowing her, I was still surprised when she agreed."

"She couldn't destroy the father of her child."

"That must have been the reason, though I didn't know it then." He was silent for a while, then he said, "It ended our friendship. We were never close again. That *thing* always hung over us like some sort of awful cloud. Even when we ended up as near neighbors we only ever met in public places with other people."

"Yes, I gathered that."

"It was a great sadness to me."

"And the secret hung over *you*, you never knew if Leonora might just say something, write something one day?"

"It was in my mind, yes."

"But she never did. She says here," I gestured towards the book, "that she never, *never*," I repeated, "would."

"I wish I'd believed that."

"I'm sure you do," I said. "Then you wouldn't have been so anxious when she said that she was writing her memoirs. Then you wouldn't have been so worried that you felt you had to silence her forever, that you had to kill her."

Chapter Twenty

Harry put his cup down so violently that the coffee splashed in the saucer.

"For God's sake, Sheila, what on earth are you saying?"

Just for a moment my confidence was shaken. Was it genuine anger, did it have the ring of outraged innocence, or was it just bluster? I looked at Harry, and something I saw in his eyes (was it fear?) made me go on.

"I think you know what I mean," I said quietly.

"Leonora died of E. coli bacteria," he said, "of polluted water. The Environment Agency people said so."

"Yes, that's right."

"So how could you imagine that she was murdered?"

"The stream was polluted. It could have been by a buildup of rotting vegetation, or animal droppings, or the carcass of a dead animal."

"That's what I mean."

"But none of those things were found."

"For heaven's sake, they would have been washed down away from the cottage."

"There were no animals in the vicinity of the stream. I've checked."

"Well, vegetable matter, then."

"I've checked that, too. It seems unlikely."

"Oh, for heaven's sake. Do you imagine that someone deliberately put a dead sheep in the stream or something?"

"Not a dead sheep. There was no need for that. You're a biochemist—I imagine it wouldn't have been difficult for you to cook up something pretty lethal in that laboratory of yours."

"That's absolutely ridiculous."

"But possible."

"My dear Sheila," Harry leaned forward and spoke slowly, as if instructing a child. "You may not know that the E. coli bacteria stays in the body for up to three days—and that's all. You may also not know that I was away in London—vouched for by a great many people—for several days before Leonora was taken ill. There is no way I could have done what you suggest."

"Yes, I did know that, about the three days. But I also know that there is a way you could have put the E. coli in the stream before you went away."

"That's nonsense. *If* such a thing had been done then, the results would have appeared earlier."

"No, not if the bacteria were enclosed in some sort of PVA water-soluble film." I was right, there *was* fear in his eyes.

"You don't know what you're talking about."

"I may not know the technical details about how it all worked, but other people—people with better scientific knowledge than I have—will be able to explain the technical details. But I do know that it was possible for you to kill Leonora like that."

There was silence for a few moments, and then he said, "Have you told this ridiculous theory to anyone else?"

"Not yet."

He seemed to relax slightly.

"Sheila, you can't really believe I could have done something like that, to Leonora, of all people!"

"You had a motive, a very strong one. You were afraid that the whole story of that Nigerian episode would come out. If it did, it wouldn't just affect you, would it? What you were really worried about was what it would do to Daphne."

"For heaven's sake . . ."

"She'd never forgive you if something disreputable from your past jeopardized her career. It would be the end of your marriage. You couldn't face that. So you had to stop Leonora. Did you go and beg her, that time you visited her just before she died? And did she punish you for what you did all those years ago, by pretending that she just *might* include that unsavory episode in her memoirs? It would have been like her to wind you up like that, knowing that she would never really do it."

I paused for a moment but he made no reply.

"And, then," I said, "when you really believed you had no choice, no other option, you devised this scheme to silence her in a way that no one would suspect."

Again he was silent, though he shook his head in denial.

"She was an old woman, living in an uncomfortable and eccentric way. It would be natural for people to think that her death had been from natural causes."

Harry got to his feet.

"This is absolutely ridiculous. I'm not going to listen to any more of it."

I got up too and stood facing him.

"But it's true, Harry, you know it is, even if you won't admit it."

"I'm admitting nothing. You have no proof to back up any of these wild accusations." His face darkened. "That's all they are, unsubstantiated accusations. And, I warn you, if you go around spreading these untruths, I'll take legal action to stop you."

"Surely," I retorted, "that would give the whole affair the very publicity you want to avoid!"

"There are other ways. I still have a great deal of influence. And let me tell you, Sheila, that if you involve Michael in this business, one way or another I'll see that his career is finished." He took a step towards me, perhaps to emphasize his point, I don't know. Tris, however, interpreted it as a threat and growled. I bent and patted him.

"It's all right, Tris, you don't have to protect me from Harry." I looked up. "Does he, Harry?"

"Don't be absurd, Sheila," he said curtly. "I have nothing more to say to you." He went towards the door. "I'll see myself out."

I didn't go to the door with him but stood there quite still. After a few minutes, Tris, worried about my immobility, whined and pawed at my skirt. I picked him up and went to the window and watched Harry's car driving away.

"Well, I don't know, Tris," I said. "I'm sure he's guilty, but how can I prove it?" Encouraged by the sound of my voice, Tris licked my face. "I think," I said, "I'd better have a word with Roger and see what he thinks."

But then, washing up the coffee cups, I thought about Harry's threat (would he have threatened me like that if he *hadn't* been guilty?) and wondered if he was really capable of making life difficult for me if I did tell Roger. Certainly there was no way I'd put Michael's career at risk. It was all very difficult and I really didn't know what to do.

It's a funny thing, but sometimes when you've been thinking about a person you suddenly run into them, and that's what happened with Roger. That afternoon I was just coming out of the chemist when I met Roger going in.

"Prescription for Jilly," he said. "Poor girl, she's got a rotten strep throat."

"How wretched for her, I'm so sorry!" Then, on an

impulse, I said, "Roger, have you got a minute? There's something I want to ask you."

"Sure." He waved the prescription. "I've got to wait for this, anyway." He went to the counter and handed it in. "Right, what is it?"

"It's a bit delicate," I said. "Could we talk somewhere else? My car's parked just around the corner."

"Now, then?" Roger shut the car door and turned to me expectantly.

So I told him about the case I'd made out against Harry, about Leonora's diary entries, Harry's laboratory, the PVA film—the lot. I told him how I'd confronted Harry and what he'd said.

"So you see," I concluded, "I know I can't prove anything, but you must admit it does all add up."

"Assuming," Roger said, "that Leonora *was* murdered."

"But . . ."

"My dear Sheila, Harry Walters was right. You've got no real evidence. Everything you've told me is purely circumstantial. I agree, you've made a very neat case, but just imagine what an even half-competent lawyer would do to it? In fact, I can't imagine it would ever come to court in the first place."

"But I'm *sure* he's guilty—if you'd seen his face! And then the way he threatened me!"

"Righteous anger on the part of an innocent man? No, I'm sorry, but there's nothing you can do and certainly nothing, I'm afraid, that the police can do."

"I see."

Roger put his hand on my arm. "I really am sorry, Sheila," he said, "but it would be wrong of me to give you false hope. I know how fond you were of Leonora, and it's only natural, given the way she died, that you should want to blame someone for her death. But I think you must accept the fact that she died—tragically and unnecessarily—of natural causes."

"I see," I said again. There seemed nothing else I could say.

"How's Thea?" Roger asked. "Everything going well?"

"Yes, she's fine. Absolutely blooming."

"That's good. Well, I'd better go and get that prescription."

"Yes, of course. Please give my love to Jilly. I do hope she's better soon."

When Roger had gone I sat in the car for a while, thinking about what he'd said. He was right, of course, I had no proof, there was nothing I could do. I knew, I really *knew* in my heart, that Harry had killed Leonora, but there was nothing that I or anyone else could do about it.

Life went on and I tried, reasonably successfully, to put the whole thing out of mind. I didn't tell Michael or Thea about my final investigations or how I had confronted Harry—the thought of his threat against Michael stopped me from doing that. We were all busy, and Thea needed my help with sorting things out at the flat, and we had pleasant shopping trips, choosing curtains and furniture for the new house.

"Mrs. Freeman said it would be all right if I took some of the china and breakable things I don't want to go in the van up to the house tomorrow," Thea said. "Completion's not until Friday, but we both thought we might as well get a move on! Could you give me a hand, do you think?"

"Of course, I'd love to. Actually, I've got those rosemary cuttings all ready for you, so they could go up there too. They're already in pots."

As usual Mrs. Freeman had the kettle on when we arrived and a fruitcake on the table.

"I made it a couple of weeks ago—all my baking things are packed up now—but they say fruitcake improves with keeping. Well, it does if you've put enough fruit and butter in it."

She cut large slices for both of us and poured the tea. "Well, isn't this cozy? I shall quite miss our little chats! Perhaps you'll both visit me when I'm up at Dulverton—I'd love to see the baby."

"I expect you'll be glad to be near your daughter," I said.

"Oh yes, and she'll be glad of me to look after little Drew now she's got this job."

"Oh, really?"

"Yes, she's helping out the new people up at Higher Croft. The lady there's opening it up as a riding center, and so Esme's going to be a sort of part-time housekeeper. They haven't moved in yet, but there's a lot to do."

"Higher Croft?" I exclaimed. "But that's where the Walters live!"

"Oh, haven't you heard? About Mr. Walters?"

"No, what's happened?"

"He had a stroke, poor man, a really bad one. Paralyzed he is, all down one side, and can't speak properly. They say he's not going to get any better, well, not at his age."

"So where is he now, why is the house sold?"

"She—that Mrs. Walters—had him put in a nursing home, down Exeter way. But she's sold up and gone to London."

"But that's terrible!"

"That's what we all said! How she could do that to the poor man! But then, she was so much younger, wasn't she? That sort of thing never works. She couldn't be bothered with an invalid, that much is certain! And as for the house, she was hardly ever there, so good riddance, we all say!"

"And has anyone been to see Mr. Walters?"

"Well, it's a fair way away, isn't it? The vicar went to see him once, and he said it was really sad the way he is now. He said he wasn't sure Mr. Walters knew who he was, and, of course, he couldn't talk or anything. Oh, well, at least there's no shortage of money there. Just as well with nursing home fees the price they are!"

"Yes," I agreed, "they're dreadful."

"She sold everything up, you know," Mrs. Freeman went on, "furniture and everything. Plenty more where that came from, I suppose!"

"Really?"

I thought of the newly decorated house and the fashionable furniture, and I thought too of Harry's laboratory. What had become of the equipment and anything else that might have been in there? Not, really, that he would have left anything incriminating, especially after our last meeting.

"Another slice of cake?" Mrs. Freeman asked and we both hurriedly made our excuses and went out to unload the things from the car.

Thea, not surprisingly, had other things on her mind and, on our way home, only made a brief reference to what Mrs. Freeman had told us about Harry, and that was mostly a strong condemnation of Daphne's behavior.

When I got home, though, I couldn't think of anything else. It suddenly occurred to me that now Marcus Bourne would never get to know his grandfather—though perhaps, under the circumstances, that was a good thing. I thought of Harry's condition and wondered, confusedly, if our confrontation had brought it on. I simply didn't know *how* I felt about that. I tried to take my mind off things by working at my computer, but either I did something wrong or it was in a bad mood because the wretched thing froze completely and I had to look up the notes Michael had given me to find a way to get out. And, when I did, it put up that smug little message about closing down incorrectly and my work being lost. I switched it off violently—(and incorrectly)—and went out into the garden to do some therapeutic weeding. I thought of Harry, until recently so vigorous and alert, struck down in that most cruel way, physically helpless, with what thoughts and frustrations and unable to communicate. And I thought of Leonora, still herself, the person—(give or take a few frailties)—she always had been, right up to the end. And I knew which fate Leonora would have chosen.

I yanked viciously at a convolvulus that was doing its best to strangle the rudbeckia, and Foss paused on his way to the orchard to poke the pile of weeds experimentally with his paw.

"The mills of God, Foss," I said, "grind slowly, yet they grind exceedingly small."

He gave me a look that might, or might not, have signified agreement and went on his way up the path.

Hazel Holt

"Sheila Malory is a most appealing heroine."
—Booklist

MRS. MALORY AND THE DELAY OF EXECUTION
0-451-20627-4

When a schoolteacher at a prestigious English prep school dies suddenly, Mrs. Malory is talked gets shanghaied into being substitute teacher with a little detecting on the side.

MRS. MALORY AND THE FATAL LEGACY
0-451-20002-0

Sheila Malory returns, this time as executor to the estate of a late, bestselling novelist. And what Malory reads into the death is a crime.

To order call: 1-800-788-6262